WITCH SNITCH

SIBÉAL POUNDER

Illustrated by
Laura Ellen
Anderson

BLOOMSBURY
LONDON OXFORD NEW YORK NEW DELHI SYDNEY

Bloomsbury Publishing, London, Oxford, New York, New Delhi and Sydney

First published in Great Britain in October 2017 by Bloomsbury Publishing Plc
50 Bedford Square, London WC1B 3DP

www.bloomsbury.com

BLOOMSBURY is a registered trademark of Bloomsbury Publishing Plc

A CIP catalogue record for this book is available from the British Library

ISBN 978 1 4088 9204 6

Typeset by RefineCatch Limited, Bungay, Suffolk
Printed and bound in Great Britain by CPI Group (UK) Ltd, Croydon CR0 4YY

1 3 5 7 9 10 8 6 4 2

For Becky, Rebecca, Robin, Tia, Madeleine (Pom)
and Flick (Cauliflower)

Hold on to your hats, above-the-pipes witches, for it is Witchoween time! Grab your jam jar bags and bejewelled dresses, brew your Clutterbucks cocktails and come on down, because the party is just about to begin!*

* There will be a place to leave your cat, should you wish to bring it.

The Weird Request

Dear Tiga,
I have a weird request for you. I need you to
present a documentary for the Fairy 5 channel
— with Fran. It's for Witchoween. Come to
Linden House tomorrow for jam and I can tell
you all about it?
Big old witchy wishes,
Peggy

'Oh good, I was wondering when Peggy was going
to do a Witchoween,' Fluffanora said, rifling
through Tiga's wardrobe. She pulled a fluffy shawl out,
wiggled her finger, and with a snap, it wrapped around
her like a skirt. 'I'd make this into a skirt if I were you.'

'What is Witchoween?' Tiga asked as she flicked through a copy of the latest *Toad* magazine.

Fluffanora flopped down on the floor next to her. 'Witchoween. You know *Witchoween*.'

Tiga looked at her blankly. 'Is it like … Halloween?'

Fluffanora and Sluggfrey, who was sliming over Tiga's boot in the corner, both rolled their eyes.

'Not really, but Halloween technically only exists because of Witchoween … and Roberta Trotter and Ruthie Soot.'

'Who?' Tiga said, taking a gulp of her Clutterbucks cocktail.

Fluffanora flicked her finger and refilled it. 'It's only one of the best and most famous witch stories! Roberta Trotter and Ruthie Soot were two teenage witches, who lived years and years and years ago – way back before Celia Crayfish. One day, they decided to sneak out of school and fly up the pipes. They'd heard so many things about the human world and they wanted to check it out.

'They took their chance on the day before Witchoween, when every witch was busy preparing for

 5

the special day, so they knew no one would notice they'd gone. Up they went until they popped out of a tiny tap in a small village on the edge of a spooky-looking forest. Of course their hats had got all tattered and pointy, plus Ruthie Soot had two very prominent warts on her nose from the pipe travel.

'The story goes, they walked through the village, barely able to see a thing apart from the pinpricks of candlelight in the windows. Ruthie Soot caught a glimpse of her reflection in one of the candlelit windows and shouted, "I'VE GOT WARTS ON MY NOSE!" So Roberta Trotter snapped back, "STOP COMPLAINING ABOUT YOUR WARTS, WART NOSE. IT'S A SMALL PRICE TO PAY FOR MISSING WITCHOWEEN. I HATE WITCHOWEEN."

'Ruthie Soot got cross and with a flick of her finger carved angry faces into a bunch of pumpkins sitting on a cart outside one of the little houses. The house belonged to a man called Jasper Gump and he sold pumpkins and all sorts of fruit and vegetables.'

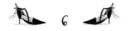

6

'Are you making this up?' Tiga said, an eyebrow raised.

Fluffanora held three fingers against her nose. 'Promise I'm not.'

(Witches do that to promise. If they're lying, their noses temporarily fall off, for twenty-four hours.)

'Continue,' Tiga said after inspecting Fluffanora's nose.

'Ruthie Soot pointed at the grumpy-looking pumpkin carvings she'd just done and said, "THIS IS HOW GRUMPY YOU'RE MAKING ME RIGHT NOW, ROBERTA! I'D RATHER BE DOING WITCHOWEEN THAN STANDING HERE WITH YOU!"

'But while they were fighting, neither of them noticed the old man who had ducked under Jasper Gump's cart for a nap. He emerged when the arguing witches were out of sight, and nearly fainted when he saw the carved pumpkins! He'd heard everything they'd said.

'"Those beings in pointy hats were magic!" he cried. "And they spoke of Halloween!"

'He completely misheard because his ears were old.

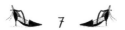

It's *Witch*oween, obviously. But he just kept shouting about *Hall*oween. He stood tall and declared to the town, "TODAY IS HALLOWEEN!" And they were all like, "Cool, sounds great." And humans have celebrated Halloween every year on that day ever since.

'That's how Halloween happened, because of Roberta Trotter and Ruthie Soot.'

'So Witchoween *is* like Halloween,' Tiga said.

'Absolutely nothing like it at all,' Fluffanora scoffed. 'Halloween is about ghosts and scary ladies in pointy hats. Witchoween is a celebration of witches! It can happen at any time, whenever you want. You just need to get your favourite witches together and celebrate how excellent you all are. Plus there's great cakes and stuff.'

'That sounds fun!' Tiga said, gulping down the last of her Clutterbucks. 'But what's Peggy's documentary got to do with Witchoween?'

'They do that every year now, for Witchoween,' Fluffanora said, getting up and rifling through Tiga's wardrobe again. 'They film a bunch of interesting

witches – it's different ones every time. It's always brilliant, because you get to find out what toothpaste they use and things like that. Fran presents it.'

'I wonder why Peggy wants me to present the documentary with Fran,' Tiga mumbled, reading the letter again.

Fluffanora shrugged. 'Who knows? She probably thinks it'll be extra special with you in it, and it'll be your first Witchoween!' She flicked her finger and one of the pillows leapt up and hit Tiga in the face. They both rolled back on to the bed in a fit of giggles.

'I'm coming with you,' Fluffanora said. 'If Peggy wants to make this documentary special, she's going to have to make me Head of Wardrobe.'

2

Fran Being Fran

Tiga and Fluffanora skipped into Linden House just in time to see Fran's eyes widen to the size of jam jar lids.

'CO-PRESENT? As in, me and ANOTHER?'

'Not just any other,' Peggy said patiently. '*Tiga.*'

'But Tiga's an AMATEUR! A garbage, rubbish, frog-face AMATEUR! No offence, Tiga.'

'None taken,' Tiga said, grabbing a pot of jam from the table and gulping down a spoonful. She was used to Fran.

'Fran,' Peggy tried again. 'Patricia the producer has specifically requested that we also include a witch presenter. She wants the documentary to include both a witch and a fairy this time.'

'I'm sure
she'd be fine
with it just being a
witch! But when it's just a
fairy, she's all – oh no, we also
need a *witch* presenter. The fairy can't do it by herself!'

Fluffanora shrugged. 'She actually makes a good point.'

'But Fran,' Peggy tried again. 'What would *Witch Snitch* be without you?'

'Why is it called *Witch Snitch*?' Tiga asked.

'No idea,' Peggy said. 'Fran made it up a long time ago, didn't you?'

Fran stuck out her chin proudly and smoothed down her beehive, letting it dramatically ping back up. 'I did, and everyone loves it. Because "snitch" means *genius* in fairy slang.'

'Does it?' Tiga asked, sounding unconvinced.

'Definitely,' Fran said. 'As an example, a while back Julie Jumbo Wings told me that she thought Crispy's hair looked like a burnt mango and so I went over to Crispy's caravan and told her that's what Julie Jumbo Wings thought. And then I fixed her hair. Later that day, Julie Jumbo Wings was looking up at Crispy's new hair, because Crispy had Julie Jumbo Wings in a head-lock, and Julie Jumbo Wings shouted over to me, "YOU LITTLE SNITCH!" And I thought, *Yes, I* am *a genius*. I am abnormally excellent at hair.'

Tiga stared at her blankly.

Peggy flopped on the sofa. 'Fran, I'll triple the budget so you can have excessive costume changes if you let Tiga present with you.'

'Deal,' Fran said, before zooming out of the window, muttering something about a hair appointment.

Peggy, Tiga and Fluffanora burst out laughing.

'That was easy,' Tiga said.

'Remember she presented *Melt My Wings and Call Me Carol*, that weird game show that involved melting her wings and calling her Carol?' Peggy said with a smile. 'She only did that because they let her dye her hair the colours of the rainbow.'

'So what do I have to do?' Tiga asked as Peggy waved her hand and a little book came cantering across the room like a badly behaved horse. It dropped to the ground halfway.

Peggy ran over and picked it up. She blew on her finger. 'I can never get that floating object finger-flick right!'

Felicity Bat levitated into the room and flicked her finger, sending the little book flying from Peggy's grasp and into Tiga's hand.

'Show-off,' Peggy whispered to Felicity Bat with a wink.

Tiga stared at the book. On the front it had a picture of a grumpy witch sitting in a bucket and the title *Berta*

Takes A Bath. 'Um ...' Tiga began. 'I'm not sure I understand why I need this.'

'Open it,' Peggy said excitedly as Tiga reluctantly did so.

Inside, it wasn't a book about a bath or a Berta at all – it was a notebook. A completely blank notebook, apart from the inside cover, which was covered in Peggy's messy handwriting.

Behind the Scenes with the Real Witches of Ritzy City
Witches to interview:

1. Miss Flint, owner of Desperate Dolls in the Docks
2. Sophia Slopp, CEO of the Mouldy Jam Factory in the Docks
3. Captain LT, boss of the Flying Ferry over Driptown
4. Melodie McDamp, Weekend Guide at the Mermaid Museum in Driptown

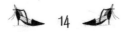

5.   Mrs Clutterbuck, owner of Clutterbucks in Ritzy City

6.   Christy Brunts, coordinator of the Costume Cupboard in Brollywood

7.   Pip Glow, actress who plays Washy Cat in Brollywood

8.   Darcy Dream, editor of *Toad* magazine in Pearl Peak

9.   Aggie Hoof, richest witch in Sinkville, in Pearl Peak

10.   Idabelle Bat, guide at the First Witch Who Landed in Sinkville historical site on the edge of Pearl Peak

11.   CONFIDENTIAL FOR SECURITY REASONS, the Cauldron Islands, Upper Cave 4

12.   Lily Cranberry, party co-host in the Coves

13.   Gretal Green, inventor at NAPA in Silver City

14.   Mrs Brew, creative director and designer at Brew's

'It's your first Witchoween notebook!' Peggy cheered. 'That's the full list of witches you and Fran need to interview. They were chosen by a panel of witches and approved by Patricia the producer in Brollywood. They sound so fun! And some of my favourites are on there.'

'What do we interview them about?' Tiga asked.

'Oh, you can ask all sorts of questions!' Peggy said, skipping about the room and tripping. 'You can film them at their place of work, ask them things like, "What advice would you give to young witches who want to do your job when they grow up?" or "Where do you buy your hats?" or –'

'What toothpaste do you use?' Fluffanora interrupted.

'Exactly,' Peggy said. 'Absolutely anything. Just get

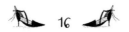

them to talk about themselves. Oh, and Patricia the producer gave you an extra assignment, Tiga. She asked that you use the notebook to write down Five Things You Didn't Know About … for each of the witches and they'll use those facts for the documentary, too!'

Tiga closed the notebook and hugged it excitedly. 'This is going to be fun! How much time have we got to do all of this?'

'Two days,' Peggy said. 'In two days I'm throwing a Witchoween – we'll need to have the documentary by then. I'll screen it at the party.'

'Two days,' Tiga said with a gulp. 'Sure … no problem.'

'And I'm sending Lizzie Beast with you,' Peggy added. 'She'll be a great camera witch.'

'And you'd be a fool not to make me Head of Wardrobe,' Fluffanora said. She flicked her finger and a ridiculously cool-looking book of dress doodles and *Toad* magazine clippings landed with a thud on top of Tiga. 'I've already been putting together some costume ideas.'

How to Make a Witchoween Journal Like Tiga's

Witchoween Journals are an essential part of the celebration. They are great for writing down party plans, interviews with your favourite witch friends and keeping a record of all your Witchoween parties throughout the years.

The largest Witchoween journal on record belongs to Melinda Zing, who has thrown 904 Witchoweens. She's nine years old.

WHAT YOU'LL NEED:

- ☆ A notebook
- ☆ Old book covers or magazines
- ☆ Scissors
- ☆ Pens
- ☆ Glue or sticky tape
- ☆ A hand that can draw a cat or something that closely resembles one

HOW TO MAKE IT:

1. The first thing you need is a notebook. And then you need to find a way to disguise it so it's a secret. There's no reason to actually disguise it these days, but we witches still do it for fun! In the olden days witches would disguise the notebooks because Celia Crayfish (the most EVIL Top Witch to ever rule Sinkville) banned Witchoween parties, so they were always held in secret. If any witch was caught with a Witchoween Journal they were in serious trouble. So find an old book cover or cut out the cover of a magazine and paste it over the front of the notebook. NOW IT'S HIDDEN.

2. Witchoween is all about celebrating other witches, so write a list of all your favourite friends. You can stick photos of them inside if you want to. It's fun to interview them and ask them Five Things You Didn't Know About them, like Tiga has to do for all the witches in the documentary.

3. Now write down these five important Witchoween questions and write down your answers, along with your witchy friends'.

☆ What is the funniest thing that has ever happened to you?

☆ If you invented a toothpaste, what would it be called?

☆ List three reasons why your best friends are brilliant.

☆ If you could only do one spell for ever, what would it be?

☆ Most witch friends have a slogan, e.g. Melinda Zing and her witches would all chant *Witches together are stronger than spells. Witches together are stronger than spells.* What is your slogan?

4. Fill pages with party ideas from this book, or your own ideas.

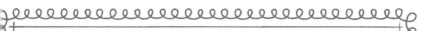

5. Witches also like to cut out pictures and articles about other witches who inspire them. Fill some pages with those who inspire you.

6. Draw a massive cat. It's essential.

TOAD MAGAZINE

Witches together are stronger than spells

3

The Docks

Later that afternoon, Tiga, Fluffanora and Lizzie Beast sat on Fluffanora's costume trunk in the Docks, next to a levitating camera, while Fran fixed her beehive of hair.

'Right,' she said. 'Let's make this one quick. We don't want to stay in the Docks longer than we have to. There's nothing to do here.'

All down the street, giant houses shaped like shoes sparkled.

'We should probably mention how Peggy made all these shoe houses when she became Top Witch,' Tiga said, flicking through her notebook. 'I love that she made houses out of bewitched shoes.'

'You should draw a cat in there,' Lizzie Beast said, prodding the notebook. 'It's essential.'

Tiga just stared at her.

'I wonder who CONFIDENTIAL is,' Fluffanora said, pointing to the eleventh witch on the list. 'Someone in the Cauldron Islands? No one's in the Cauldron Islands at this time of year!'

'It must be someone really important,' Lizzie Beast grunted.

Tiga wrinkled her nose. 'But even Peggy is mentioned by name on this list and she's Top Witch! Who's more important than that?'

'Well, the witch is probably *called* Confidential for Security Reasons,' Fran said grandly. 'That's the most likely explanation.'

'It's really not,' Tiga, Fluffanora and Lizzie Beast all said at once.

'I'll do a practice take,' Fran said, clearing her throat loudly. 'You are about to learn a lot about TV, Tiga. Oooooh WEEEEE oooooh WEEEEEE, blubber blubber WEEEEEEE.'

'What's she doing?' Lizzie Beast asked nervously as her camera fell to the ground with a bang. She hastily picked it up.

'Show business WEEEEEE,' Fran said as she spun in the air, a huge grin on her face. 'Welcome to *Witch Snitch! The Inside Scoop on the Real Witches of Ritzy City!* It's a Witchoween tradition, and what a tradition it is! In this special show, featuring me and my dear witch friend Tiga, we'll introduce you to some of Sinkville's most interesting, exciting and weird witches! So here's to Witchoween! Raise a glass of Clutterbucks to all the wonderful witches – AND FAIRIES.'

She looked really intently into the camera.

'Did you get that?' she asked Lizzie Beast.

Lizzie Beast shifted awkwardly on her feet.

'You said you were going to do a practice take,' Tiga pointed out.

'YOU STILL FILM A PRACTICE TAKE!' Fran shouted. 'New skirt,' she said, clicking her fingers at Fluffanora.

24

Fluffanora pulled a tiny tutu out of her trunk, and with a flick of her finger, it was on Fran.

Fran nodded approvingly. 'Like it. Right, now, we begin. Tiga, come and stand next to me. It's probably best if you look at me adoringly.'

Tiga reluctantly trudged over to where Fran was hovering.

Fran narrowed her eyes. 'Camera witch!'

'Right, yes,' Lizzie Beast grunted. 'Five, four, three, two, one – and go!'

Fran stared at her blankly. 'Five, four, three, two, one and go? Lizzie Beast, we are not an egg-and-spoon race.'

'Fran,' Tiga began.

'It should be – Fran's fabulous documentary, take one – aaaaand ACTION!'

'You knew what I meant,' Lizzie Beast mumbled under her breath.

'My skirt is wilting! Waaaaardrrrrooobe! This is what happens when you get it wrong, Lizzie Beast. Wilting skirt! Wilting skirt!' Fran cried, waving her hands at Fluffanora.

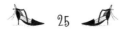

Fluffanora turned to Tiga. 'I'm going to squash her. Quick, turn my hands to jelly so I physically can't, it's the only way to stop me. RENDER MY HANDS WOBBLY AND USELESS, QUICK, DO IT NOW!' Fluffanora roared mockingly. 'BEFORE IT'S TOO LATE!'

'Oh, you're both as dramatic as each other,' Tiga said.

'FIX MY SKIRT, WARDROBE!' Fran bellowed, as Fluffanora flicked her finger and sent an electric shock through Fran's skirt.

'WELCOME TO *WITCH SNITCH*,' Fran said in a voice so high Tiga could barely hear her.

'We'll need to let that electric shock wear off,' Lizzie Beast said, putting the lens back on the camera.

SOME TIME LATER ...

Tiga snorted as Lizzie Beast shook her awake.

'Fran's voice isn't dangerous any more,' Lizzie Beast grunted, pointing over at the little fairy, who looked like she was doing warm-up stretches.

'Great,' Tiga muttered, pulling herself out of

Fluffanora's trunk. Fluffanora was perched on the side of it sipping a Clutterbucks.

'Now we'll film Miss Flint, the first witch on the list!' Fran said, narrowing her eyes. 'Since Tiga has awoken from her lengthy nap.'

Lizzie Beast readied the camera. Fran knocked on the door to Desperate Dolls.

The curtains twitched slightly, there was a scuffle inside and then BOOM, the door swung open!

'Miss … Flint?' Fran said, choking on the words.

'HELLO! I'M READY FOR MY INTERVIEW!'

Miss Flint looked different.

'I thought I'd spruce myself up for the show,' she said. 'So I put on a little bit of make-up.'

Her eyebrows looked like curled-up cats. Her teeth were stained with the plum purple colour painted on her lips. Her fake eyelashes were hanging off.

'Miss Flint,' Fluffanora said, squeezing the old witch's arm. 'This is a show about how brilliant and interesting you are, how incredible your business is, your accomplishments! You didn't need to spruce yourself up – it

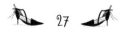

doesn't matter one bit what your face looks like!'

'Which is just as well,' Fran said, kicking one of the fake eyelashes. 'Because we don't have time to fix this.'

'I wonder if you could help me make some embellished dresses for the dolls? I said I'd send some up to my friend Delia at Delia's Dolls – she has a secret shop above the pipes,' Miss Flint said. 'We could work on them as you interview me.'

'Of course,' Tiga said. 'I've always wanted to know how to add cool embellishments – we could use the designs as inspiration for our Witchoween outfits.'

☆⭐☆

Tiga sat patiently while Fran fiddled with the lighting around Miss Flint. 'Maybe a little to the left ... OH FROGS, NO!'

Fluffanora put her head in her hands.

'Lizzie Beast, roll the camera!'

Tiga put her arm around Miss Flint. 'I'm sorry about her,' she whispered. 'She's being more Fran than I've ever seen Fran being.'

28

'Don't worry,' Miss Flint said kindly. 'I can't hear a word she's saying. She's too small for my bad ears.'

'And ACTION,' shouted Lizzie Beast.

'Here we are,' Fran said, waving a hand across Miss Flint's face, 'in the famous Desperate Dolls shop. The shop was made famous because it was one of the stops in Witch Wars and hid a clue that would see the contestants travel to the Coves. And this here is the witch behind the magic! Miss Flint –' She stopped. 'I'm sorry, but the whole … face situation you have going on is very distracting.'

'Oh, get on with it!' Fluffanora said, flicking her finger slyly and giving Fran the exact same makeover. 'Now there's two of you, so it looks deliberate,' she said with a satisfied smile.

'Miss Flint,' Fran said through gritted teeth and a lot of lipstick. 'How did you get into fixing creepy dolls?'

Miss Flint scrunched up her face. 'I can't really hear y–'

Tiga leaned over and helpfully whispered the question in her ear.

'Well … Um … That's a good question … well …' Miss Flint said, tapping her chin.

'Be a bit quicker,' Fran said impatiently. 'If you don't speak quickly we'll have to cut you out.'

'Well,' Miss Flint went on. 'I thought it was a waste not to fix them; better to find them a new home.'

'Right,' Fran said, not really listening. 'What's the most desperate doll you've ever fixed?'

Tiga whispered the question in Miss Flint's ear.

'Tiga, stop moving,' Fran hissed.

'Well … um …' Miss Flint said. 'That's a good question.'

'Quicker,' Fran said bossily, then looked apologetically

into the camera lens and mouthed, 'Sorry, viewers.'

'Well … um …' Miss Flint said.

'This is television, Miss Flint,' Fran said, tapping her foot in the air. 'You've got to be quicker.'

'Oh, I know,' Miss Flint finally said. 'There was one doll with a bat living in it. Every so often it would stick its wings out of the doll's ears and fly around, terrifying everyone. I had to agree to give the bat my house just to get it out of there. I live in the shop now.'

'And how many dolls do you sell per week?' Fran asked quickly.

'NoneIhardlyeversellany,' Miss Flint replied before Tiga could whisper the question in her ear.

'Fran,' Tiga said, holding up her hand so she covered the camera lens. 'Did you just do a *fast speaking* spell on Miss Flint?'

'What makes you say that?!' Fran asked.

Smoke started coming out of Miss Flint's mouth.

'Mytonguefeelslikeit'sahelicopter!'

Fran began whistling innocently.

'And cut,' Lizzie Beast said with a sigh.

Five Things You Didn't Know About Miss Flint, by Tiga

1. Her first name is Gregette.

2. She studied Moth, a rare and virtually extinct witch language, at Waverly Way College.

3. In Celia Crayfish's memoirs she describes Miss Flint as having 'a heart of gold and the aroma of a soft cheese'.

4. She has an extra toe, which she calls Mini Gregette.

5. She once appeared on an episode of Fran's failed show, *Melt My Wings and Call Me Carol*, as the witch who had to shout 'CAROL! CAROL! I'M CALLING YOU CAROL!' She didn't enjoy it.

How to Embellish a Fabulous Witchoween Outfit (Inspired by Desperate Dolls)

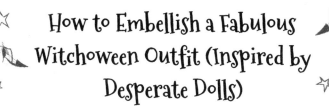

☆ Transform a simple T-shirt by placing some stick-on gems in a collar shape around the neckline, or glue them in a long loop, like a hanging necklace.

☆ Pom-poms (small or large) are a great addition to any outfit – and have been a popular outfit embellishment at Witchoween parties for centuries. Glue a line of pom-poms around the waist or hem of a skirt for classic Witchoween style.

☆ Ask some older witches in your house if they have any old bits of broken jewellery, beads, patches of fabric, odds and ends, that they don't want and sew them on to your skirt. This is a Witchoween tradition that young witches still do today. You can create all sorts of interesting and eclectic designs!

Jam Factory

Next on the list was Sophia Slopp at the Mouldy Jam Factory, which was conveniently just a short hop across the road from Desperate Dolls.

Inside, the mouldy jam factory walls were covered with pictures of Mavis's face.

'Mavis is our number one supplier of mouldy jam,' Sophia Slopp explained. She was much younger than Tiga had imagined, maybe only a couple of years older than Tiga and her friends. She had long hair tied into two flowing bunches on either side of her head, and wore a pair of baggy dungarees splattered with jam.

'The jam on Mavis's stall,' Sophia Slopp went on, 'is always going mouldy. Plus she loves cats, so she likes

the idea of 'em being fed. Once we sent her a couple of pots of our best mouldy-jam cat food, called *MEOW-OULD*, and she told us a very funny story about how she accidentally sold them as normal jam to that Mrs Brew, the fashion designer.'

'That's Fluffanora's mum,' Fran said, as Tiga turned to see Fluffanora frantically scrubbing her tongue with a spare sparkly Fran-sized skirt.

'Oh, you ate it,' Sophia Slopp said, looking slightly embarrassed. 'But you lived! So that's something. I hear mouldy jam tastes almost identical to non-mouldy jam, it's just a bit … fuzzier.'

Fluffanora's face turned green.

'Ah,' Sophia Slopp said. 'That reminds me. I was hoping you could help me with something. I'm planning to launch a new flavour of jam cat food and I'm completely stuck for ideas! Do you have any?'

'Parrot,' Fran said. 'Melon! Garden!'

Everyone stared at Fran.

'All … excellent, um, suggestions,' Sophia Slopp said kindly as she pretended to write them down.

'Right,' Fran said, clapping her hands. 'Now we've got that sorted, let's get this interview in the can. We'll film over here.'

She floated over to a swimming-pool-sized vat of jam with a thick film of mould on the top.

Sophia Slopp nodded and handed Tiga a pile of star-shaped sunglasses. 'You need to wear protective goggles near the mouldy jam vats.'

'But these are *sunglasses*, not goggles,' Tiga said, looking from the disgusting gloopy pool to Sophia Slopp and back again.

'Untrue,' Sophia Slopp said, pointing at a tiny description on the side of the glasses.

These are MOULDY JAM PROTECTION GLASSES, invented by Mavis.

'Well, *that's* hardly comforting,' Tiga said as she handed a pair of the glasses to Fluffanora, who handed them to Lizzie Beast, who tried to hand them on to Fran, but instead pinged her –

INTO THE MOULDY VAT OF JAM.

'Oh dear, I didn't mean t–' Lizzie Beast began, as Fluffanora high-fived her.

'Well played,' Fluffanora said. 'Well played.'

'FRAN!' Tiga cried, peering into the vat. She couldn't see her in amongst all the gloopy bits!

'Is that her?' Fluffanora said casually. 'Oh, no. That's some vibrant mould.'

Tiga rolled up her sleeve and dunked an arm in. She felt around in the gloop. Lizzie Beast and Sophia Slopp joined in too.

'She'll be *fine*,' Fluffanora said. 'Give her a moment or two to resurface …'

'Put your arms in!' Tiga ordered.

'I didn't sign up for this,' Fluffanora said, flicking her finger, and with a thud and a bit of magic, a giant pair of rubber gloves appeared. She pulled them on and plunged a hand in too.

Tiga felt around frantically in the gloop. 'Fran!' she shouted. 'Fran!'

'I'VE GOT HER,' Lizzie Beast shouted, making the

mouldy jam wobble. She pulled a tiny thing out triumphantly and shook it off.

They all looked up at it eagerly.

'It's … a tiny doll,' Tiga said.

'That happens sometimes,' Sophie Slopp said. 'Miss Flint's got a strong arm, and sometimes she thinks she's throwing the dolls into a pile ready for sorting, but she's actually throwing them across the road and in here.'

Fluffanora pulled another tiny thing out of the gloop. 'Another doll!'

'I have something!' Sophie Slopp said with a snort. 'Oh, no. Just another doll.'

'How many tiny dolls are in here?' Tiga cried, just as she wrapped her fingers around something wriggling. 'Wait! I've got her!'

It was Fran, smeared in slime. Tiga gently placed her like a limp fish on the floor.

'WE SHALL NEVER SPEAK OF THIS AGAIN,' Fran said sternly.

The others nodded.

'Of course not,' Fluffanora said, trying not to smile.

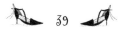

'Wait a second!' Sophia Slopp cried. 'Why is the mouldy jam sparkling?'

Fran squeezed some mouldy jam juice out of her beehive. 'I panicked,' she said. 'The glittery dust just … fell out of my armpits. I was scared! It could happen to anyone.'

Sophia Slopp stuck a finger in the jam and put it in her mouth, making a sucking noise.

'Gross,' Fluffanora whispered in Tiga's ear.

'It's delicious! It's the perfect new taste I was looking for – mouldy jam cat food, with a mild fairy flavour!'

'I'm not sure we should encourage the cats to eat fai–' Fran began, but Sophia Slopp was squealing so loudly it drowned her out.

'IT'S PERFECT. FRAN, YOU ARE A GENIUS!'

Fran stuck her nose in the air. 'I think you'll find it's *snitch*.'

Five Things You Didn't Know About Sophia Slopp, by Tiga

1. She got the idea for mouldy jam cat food when she was five years old.

2. Because of her and the food she provides, the cat population of Sinkville has quadrupled over the past five years.

3. Her jam cat food is the bestselling cat food in Sinkville.

4. She won the award for 'Nicest Witch EVER to Cats'.

5. She hates cats.

How to Play the Mouldy Jam Dive Party Game

NOTE: This game is disgusting. But also fun. But definitely disgusting.

WHAT YOU'LL NEED:

- ☆ A lot of red jelly (and water to make the jelly)
- ☆ A gigantic bowl!
- ☆ Cotton wool (a clump of it)
- ☆ Tiny dolls, or you can make your own
- ☆ A tiny notebook (make your own by folding over tiny sheets of paper and designing your own cover)
- ☆ Glitter glue
- ☆ Sunglasses (the weirder the better)
- ☆ Glitter (mild fairy flavour)

HOW TO MAKE IT:

1. Make the jelly, and once it's set, *reeeeally* scrunch it with your hands in the big bowl.

2. Add the clumps of cotton wool and really scrunch that in too. The cotton wool will represent the mould, because none of us have time to sit around waiting for your jam to go mouldy.

3. Drop in the tiny dolls and hide them, BUT keep hold of one.

4. Cover the chosen doll's skirt in glitter glue. This fairy represents Fran. If you have time, you can add a beehive to her head using some grey wool.

5. Add Fran (once her skirt has dried) to the bowl, along with the notebook and hide them.

6. PUT ON YOUR SUNGLASSES.

HOW TO PLAY:

★ Each competitor takes it in turns to dive a hand in and try to find Fran and/or the notebook.

★ Players must keep their eyes closed when they dive their hand into the bowl.

☆ The winners are those who find either Fran or the notebook. ULTIMATE WITCH WINNING POINTS IF YOU FIND BOTH.

☆ (Make sure <u>no</u> small witches eat the jelly afterwards. The cotton-wool mould is <u>not</u> edible.)

5

The Flying Ferry

Despite the jam factory fiasco, Fran's mood lifted significantly the closer the four of them got to the Flying Ferry. They were only at the edge of the docks and the fairy was already close to exploding.

'IT'S MY FAVOURITE THING TO DO AT WEEKENDS!' she roared. The Flying Ferry, she'd told them, took off from a hidden spot on Sunken Ship Road.

'I remember visiting the spa there during Witch Wars,' Tiga said. 'You tried to slip into a fish, Fran.'

'Ah, memories!' Fran said, pinching her cheek. 'Now, we just need to get down there.'

'And how are we going to do that?' Tiga stared into the glossy black water. She could see the pinpricks of light from Waverly Way below.

'IN THE TRUNK, THANK YOU,' Fran said, magically lifting up the trunk and then, with the full power of her tiny body, shoving Lizzie Beast in head first. Much to Tiga's surprise, Lizzie Beast disappeared completely.

'But we can't all fit in there!' Tiga cried as she raced over to the trunk to inspect it. 'How did Lizzie Beast fit?'

'IN!' Fran demanded.

☆⭐☆

The inside of the trunk looked like a really well accessorised submarine. Fluffanora's handmade necklaces and tiny skirts for Fran hung on rails along the walls, and the seats Lizzie Beast and Fluffanora were perched on were strewn with tiny fairy shoes, and a couple of bigger, Tiga-sized ones.

Tiga could feel the thing wobbling through the air, followed by a strange splosh as they hit the water.

'How did we fit in here?' Tiga asked.

'Simple shrink spell,' Lizzie Beast said. 'All you need is some fairy dust and the ability to shout.'

'It's scary how much power she has,' Fluffanora said

as she parted a rail of tiny skirts and peeked out of a porthole. Tiga could just make out the ghostly-looking sunken boats of Sunken Ship Road in the distance. And Fran up ahead in her swimming costume.

Down and down the trunk went, until it was brushing the tips of the sunken ships and Lizzie Beast was green from seasickness. There was a bang, and the trunk swirled around in a black ink-like substance.

'I can't see!' Fluffanora cried. 'What's happening?!'

Tiga grabbed hold of Lizzie Beast and covered her face. There was a thud as the trunk rolled and came to a stop on firm ground.

'Do you think we've hit the seabed?' Fluffanora asked.

The trunk popped open. 'NO! YOU'RE ABOARD THE FLYING FERRY!'

Tiga snapped her head up in amazement. There, hovering over the trunk, was a gigantic, grinning –

'LUCY TATTY?!' Tiga cried.

'Ahoy, me witches! Tiga, I'm your number one fan!' she said, reaching a giant hand into the trunk as Tiga SCREAMED.

48

'Who's that?' Lizzie Beast whispered to Fluffanora.

'Oh,' Fluffanora said with a smile. 'That's Lucy Tatty. She's little and lives in Silver City, just down the road from Tiga. She's obsessed with Witch Wars and Tiga was her favourite contestant. She watched all the episodes on Fairy 5 and now low-level stalks Tiga. And dresses like her. And makes her weird presents out of cat hair.'

'Lucy Tatty?' Tiga finally managed to say once she'd composed herself. 'But ... but it says Captain LT in the notebook.' She ran a finger down the list. 'It definitely says Captain LT.'

'Aaargh, me witchies, that's my sailing name!' Lucy Tatty said, punching Tiga's arm. 'Get it, LT, Lucy Tatty. And then I added Captain!'

The ship was docked underwater, but protected by a strange bubble that kept the water out. It was a gigantic hulk of a vessel, painted in gorgeous glossy black with portholes that glowed brightly.

There was a creaking sound as it started to rise up to the surface. Lucy Tatty stood on the bow, her hands in the air.

'LIFT-OFF!' she screamed as they hit the surface and the bubble popped. The ship lurched up out of the water and into the air! It glided along, weaving between all the rusty pipes hanging over Sinkville.

Tiga wrapped herself around a rail as the boat rocked enthusiastically from left to right. 'No one told me it was going to fly!' she cried.

'It's called the *Flying* Ferry,' all of them said at once.

'I thought it was just called that because it sounded nice!' Tiga shouted as the ship dived to the left to avoid a particularly chunky hanging pipe.

'I want a sailing name like Lucy Tatty,' Fran said. 'I know … I can be Captain … Fabulous. Yes! CAPTAIN FABULOUS!'

'Terrifying,' Fluffanora said mockingly. 'That'll scare off the pirates.'

'It might confuse them enough to keep them away,' Lucy Tatty said seriously.

'Wait, *what*?' Fluffanora spluttered. 'There are *pirates* up here?'

'No,' Lucy Tatty said, turning the wheel. 'Mostly just

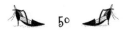

rogue human toothbrushes that fall down the pipes.'

One pinged off the bow of the boat and knocked Fran sideways.

'See. I like to call them pirates.'

'How long have you worked on the Flying Ferry?' Tiga asked as Lizzie Beast started rolling the camera.

'Oh, I don't really,' Lucy Tatty said.

Tiga raised an eyebrow as Fran hovered around Lucy Tatty, trying to take over the interview.

'Lucy Tatty,' Fran said into the camera, 'is one of our Witchoween witches because she took a school trip on the Flying Ferry, which flies by itself, and she thought it was a shame that there wasn't a captain to greet witches when they boarded.'

'So you just sit on the Flying Ferry and talk to the witches who travel on it?' Tiga asked. 'That's really lovely of you.'

Lucy Tatty nodded. 'But not only that, Tiga, I also MAKE THINGS.'

'Oh really,' Tiga said, a lump of worry in her voice.

'What kind of things, Lucy?' Fluffanora asked.

'NO TALKING FROM WARDROBE!' Fran shouted, shooing her away.

'Well, I'm glad you're here,' Lucy Tatty said, rubbing her little hands together. 'Because I wanted to reveal my latest project for the first time, on camera, in front of you, Tiga! And I would love your feedback, because I think it's not quite ready and needs a few tweaks.'

'What does?' Tiga asked nervously.

The Flying Ferry swung to the left.

'THIS!' Lucy Tatty roared, waving her arms madly at what hovered up ahead.

Fluffanora stifled a snort. 'Brilliant.'

Up ahead, standing proud in the clouds, was a giant painted cardboard cut-out of Tiga's face. The mouth was open, creating a giant hole.

'Are we going to fly –' Tiga began as the ferry dived through cardboard Tiga's mouth, knocking out a couple of teeth.

Tiga peered over the bow of the boat and watched as the teeth landed in the water below.

'So …' Lucy Tatty said excitedly. 'What do you think?'

'AND CUT,' Fran shouted, rather annoyed it wasn't her face.

'Well, this is very pleasant,' Fluffanora said, after Lucy Tatty bounded off to the back of the boat. 'Peace and quiet.' She reached into her trunk and pulled out a tray of Clutterbucks. The four of them nestled on the bow and watched Sinkville pass by beneath them.

'I can't believe I didn't know about the Flying Ferry,' Tiga said. 'Has it been around long?'

Fran lowered her whole body into Fluffanora's Clutterbucks drink like it was a hot bath. 'Oh, the Flying Ferry was very important back in the day. Every hundred years, the mermaid queen would visit Sinkville. She'd emerge from a pipe in Driptown and then she'd be placed in the ceremonial bathtub, wheeled to the Flying Ferry and whisked off to the Docks, where she was collected by a troop of fairies and flown, still in the bathtub, to Linden House for her meeting with the Top Witch.'

'Mermaids?' Tiga said. 'Mermaids are *real*?'

Fran turned towards Lizzie Beast and whispered,

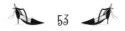

'Sometimes I worry about her … if a fairy tells you mermaids exist, then mermaids exist.'

'I just thought they were made up,' Tiga mumbled.

'You thought that about witches too, once,' Fluffanora said with a wink.

'Anyway,' Fran went on. 'Almost no witches would choose to travel on the Flying Ferry – they'd choose any other mode of transport before this one, even if it is the fastest way to the mermaid museum.'

Tiga looked around her. The Flying Ferry was completely empty. The boat tipped to the left and Tiga could see thousands of low-hanging pipes in the distance, all dripping loudly. The Flying Ferry creaked again.

'And why would witches rather choose any mode of transport other than this one?' she asked slowly.

Fran grabbed Fluffanora's finger and used it like a back scrubber. 'Because of this bit.'

'This bi–' Tiga began, just as the Flying Ferry shot upwards! It soared higher and higher. Tiga clung frantically to the side of the boat to stop herself falling off completely. Lizzie Beast grabbed Fluffanora and the

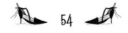

54

trunk and wedged her feet
into a railing, hanging like a
monkey with exceptionally
long hair. Fran continued
to bathe in the Clutterbucks
cocktail in Fluffanora's hand.

'They find it terrifying!' Fran
shouted as the ship flipped
forward and nosedived towards a
large, open pipe! They were moving
so fast Tiga felt like her hair was five
minutes behind her.

With a loud sucking noise, the ship
plummeted into darkness. Tiga felt sick
as they tore through the pipe at break-
neck speed.

'DON'T LET ME GO, LIZZIE!'
Fluffanora shouted through the darkness.

'Or the trunk,' Tiga heard Fran say. 'This
documentary would be nothing without my
costume changes.'

The ferry landed with an almighty SPLOSH in a perfectly still pool of water.

'AND WE'RE HERE!' Fran said – just as Fluffanora threw up in her trunk.

Five Things You Didn't Know About Lucy Tatty, by Tiga

1. She's currently writing a Witch Wars fanzine: *Tigazine*.

2. She invented a small, round cheese-water-flavoured sweet called Tigabits – a nod to Tiga's time above the pipes living in the human world, and the fact her evil guardian Miss Heks only fed her cheese water.

3. She has a small pet slug called Tiga.

4. She makes her own clothes so she can look just like Tiga.

5. She has discovered cats *really* like Tigabits.

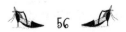

How to Play Pin the Tooth on the Tiga

1. Print out a picture of Tiga's face (or you can use a photo of a family member).

2. Draw a bunch of teeth (one for each of your guests), and carefully cut them out.

3. Add something to help them stick (a strip of sticky tape, for example).

4. Guests are then blindfolded one at a time and have to stick the tooth as close to Tiga's mouth as possible.

5. The winner gets a prize. It is customary at Witchoween parties that the winners of any games get to put their faces in the largest cake. These days witches tend to prefer just an extra-large slice.

6

The Mermaid Museum

The pool that the Flying Ferry had landed in was conveniently only a short swim to the entrance of the Mermaid Museum, which was framed by two gigantic, glistening mermaid tails.

Tiga bobbed in the water in front of it. 'So cool,' she said, just as a multicoloured flash shot past, making her jump. She blinked and spun around desperately looking for it. There it was again!

'Is that ... a *mermaid*?' she whispered to Fran.

'Don't be ridiculous, Tiga. It's a magic incantation of a mermaid. It's the mermaid *museum*, not the sea above the pipes.'

'Oh,' Tiga said, feeling silly. 'I thought there might be real mermaids in the mermaid museum.'

'We're not cruel,' Fran said with a tut. 'And anyway, they swim too fast to catch.'

'So they live in the sea above the pipes?' Tiga asked.

Fran nodded just as the great glass door to the museum opened and the insides lit up to welcome them. 'The ones we know about live in a place called the Hidden Lagoon.'

'Wow,' Fluffanora said, leaping off her trunk and into the water. She leaned over and tapped Tiga's bottom jaw, closing it and stopping the unnecessary dribble.

Tiga wiped her chin.

'Incredible,' she whispered, her eyes wide. She climbed on to a platform with the others and was blasted with some warm air.

'Dryer spell,' Fluffanora said knowingly.

'Look at the replica of the Hidden Lagoon. Isn't it wonderful?' Fran said.

Tiga tried to take it all in. The model of the lagoon was huge and encased in a glass tank, with brightly lit cities. A big red one called Lobstertown, one filled with old yachts and shipping containers called Anchor Rock,

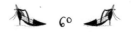

a gorgeously ornate town covered in shells.

'Big fan of Swirlyshell,' Fluffanora said with a nod.

'I like the look of Hammerhead Heights,' Tiga said, eyeing the messy-looking city teeming with sharks. She had a huge smile smacked on her face as she watched holograms of mermaids weave in and out of the sparkling cities.

A portly mermaid with bright green glossy hair emerged from the water beside the platform and bowed politely. 'Welcome to the Mermaid Museum.'

'What about her?' Tiga mumbled out of the corner of her mouth. 'Is she real?'

Fran floated right through her face. 'Another hologram.'

The mermaid hologram felt at the fairy-sized hole she now had in her cheek.

'FRAN!' came a moany voice. 'FOR THE LAST *TIME*, STOP FLYING THROUGH THE MERMAID HOLOGRAMS AND PUTTING HOLES IN THEM! THEY ARE RIDICULOUSLY EXPENSIVE TO REPLACE!'

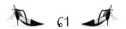

Fran turned to the camera and smiled. 'Melodie McDamp loves me.'

Melodie McDamp was in charge of the mermaid museum at weekends. She was a teenager, dressed in mermaid-print leggings and chewing on Bubbly Bat gum like she didn't want to be there. Her hair was plaited down one side and she wore a pearl-studded crown on her head.

'Oh good, you're here,' she said, blowing a bubble. She flicked her finger and popped it. 'I need your help. I have a bunch of tiny witches arriving in five minutes and I need to dress you up as mermaids.'

'We'll film it!' Fran said. 'This will be great. Melodie, you can talk a little about the mermaids.' She turned to Tiga. 'Melodie was chosen for this documentary because she knows more about mermaids than any other witch in Sinkville.'

Melodie McDamp sighed and blew another bubble. Fran popped it with a kick.

'AND ACTION!'

Tiga slipped her legs into a glistening purple tail while Fluffanora wriggled into one shaped like a lobster's.

'The Hidden Lagoon features a number of exciting mermaid cities,' Melodie McDamp said, pointing at a map.

'ZOOM!' Fran shouted at Lizzie Beast. 'ZOOM THE CAMERA.'

Lizzie Beast was finding it difficult to balance in the shark tail she was wearing.

Fluffanora rolled her eyes, which seemed to be enough to unbalance the lobster tail costume, and she tipped right over.

'There is the ancient capital, Swirlyshell, which is where the mermaid queen lives,' Melodie explained. 'Then you have Anchor Rock in the north, where mermaids live in old sunken boats and upcycled shipping containers. In the south is Oysterdale, where fancy mermaids live in even fancier sandcastles, and in the west is Lobstertown, the coolest mermaid city. They paint whales there and call it art, and they have a famous cartoon called *Clippee*, the cartoon lobster in a dress. And finally in the east is Hammerhead Heights,

a mammoth city made from towering rock towers and infested with sharks.'

Tiga shivered.

'Every one hundred years, the mermaid queen visits the Top Witch at Linden House. Witches and mermaids have coexisted peacefully for thousands of years.'

'The crowds go wild as the fancy mermaid in a bathtub is pushed down Ritzy Avenue,' Fran said, winking at the camera. 'Everyone makes this very special witch bunting and we hang it all over Sinkville.' She floated up to the black bunting hanging overhead.

'So which pipe goes to the Hidden Lagoon?' Tiga asked, staring into one. It was pitch black.

'We don't know, and unfortunately, there are 103,994 pipes in Driptown, and no one can be bothered to check them all. Who knows where you might end up if you got the wrong one?' Melodie said straight into the camera.

'Just think,' Fluffanora said, attempting to swish her tail and falling into Lizzie Beast. 'There are mermaids our age swimming about in that lagoon. Groups of mermaid friends, just like us – but *mermaids*. I bet they're *really* cool.'

'And slimy,' Lizzie Beast added.

'We should find the pipe and go there. I bet *we* can find it,' Fluffanora said, determinedly hopping over to one of the pipes. 'Bet it's this one.'

'Ah ah ah,' Melodie said, flicking her finger and making Fluffanora stand upright again.

'I'm not a puppet,' Fluffanora said grumpily as she tried to shake free of Melodie's spell.

'No, you're a witch,' Fran said. 'And witches do not go swimming about in human oceans in search of hidden lagoons. Now, let's have a crab cream shake.' She wiggled her nose and a giant shell landed in Tiga's hand, filled with strange bubbling liquid.

'CHEERS!' Fran said, clicking her tiny shell against Tiga's and downing her drink in one. 'FROGS, THAT'S DISGUSTING!' she roared. 'AND CUT!'

As they swam out of the mermaid museum, there was an almighty bang. Tiga spun around and there, neatly on top of Fluffanora's floating trunk,

was the latest issue of *Toad* magazine.

Fluffanora began flicking through it. '*Ugh*, I hate it when they write about me.'

Fran swooped down from above and splatted on the page. 'Oooh, not just about you – about *all of us*!'

TOAD MAGAZINE

SINKVILLE IN THE SPOTLIGHT!

Our favourite Witch Wars duo, Tiga and her irritating fairy Fran, plus the forever fashionable and oh-so-entertaining Fluffanora, and that tall one with the long hair, are making this year's documentary for Peggy Pigwiggle's first official Top Witch Witchoween! It'll feature some impressive and interesting witches, plus comedy scenes – including Fran drowning in a vat of mouldy jam! Our favourite *Toad* spy is keeping a close eye on them, so stay tuned for more gossip.

They all looked nervously at Fran, apart from Fluffanora, who was trying not to laugh.

'The bit about the mouldy jam,' Tiga began. 'I'm sure you could tell people it wasn't yo–'

'WE NEVER SPEAK OF IT!' Fran interrupted. 'Now, where is this *Toad* spy?'

They all looked around. Driptown was perfectly quiet, apart from the occasional dripping of the pipes and the groans from the old steel boats anchored nearby.

The place was empty. No one had been following them.

'AH HA!' Fran cried, racing over to Lizzie Beast's hat and pointing madly. 'THERE IT IS!'

'Lizzie Beast's hat?' Fluffanora said, an eyebrow raised. 'You do know *hats* can't spy, Fran?'

'I think you're being mean to Lizzie Beast,' Tiga added.

Lizzie Beast, smartly, stayed still and silent.

'NO, YOU SILLY WITCHES,' Fran said as she landed on the hat and struggled backwards, her arms

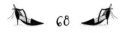

bowed like she was trying to lift something. 'IT'S A MICRO CAT!'

'A WHAT?!' they all cried, apart from Lizzie Beast, who didn't dare to move or speak.

Tiga moved closer, to see what Fran was wrestling with.

'Very rare,' Fran said. 'They invented them for fairies years ago. Because fairies campaigned to be allowed to have the same pets as witches. But then a load of fairies got eaten by their normal-sized cats, who mistook them for flies, and so a witch named Fifi Fluff invented *the micro cat* – a spell-shrunken version of a regular cat.'

'I should be surprised,' Tiga said. 'And yet, I'm not.'

'That's because you're a weird witch like us now,' Fluffanora said, giving Tiga a nudge.

'And they can run really fast when not wearing a collar,' Fran said. 'It could report back to *Toad* magazine headquarters all the way in Pearl Peak from here in a mere few minutes!'

Lizzie Beast focused the camera on the tiny thing.

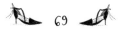

Fran attached a glittery collar and lead to it, and with a flick of her finger soared off up high with it. It looked irritated.

'WE'LL TAKE IT WITH US,' she shouted down to Tiga. 'THAT WAY IT CAN'T REPORT BACK TO *TOAD* MAGAZINE.'

'Where next?' Fluffanora asked.

Tiga flicked through her notebook. 'TO CLUTTER-BUCKS!' she cried, as a bunch of Clutterbucks cocktails obediently leapt from the trunk, completely soaking Fluffanora.

Five Things You Didn't Know About Melodie McDamp, by Tiga

1. Melodie McDamp knows which pipe leads to the Hidden Lagoon.

2. Melodie's middle name is Coddelia.

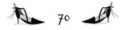

3. She is best friends with Idabelle Bat, who works at the First Witch Who Landed in Sinkville historical site on weekends.

4. She's originally from Pearl Peak, although her family moved to Driptown to live on a boat.

5. She owns a hundred and four pairs of mermaid-print leggings.

How to Make Witch Bunting

Make no mistake: witch bunting is very different from human bunting – mostly because it is ninety per cent edible. The more edible things you put on witch bunting, the better your bunting will be.

WHAT YOU'LL NEED:

- ☆ You'll need to be a witch
- ☆ Your witch hat
- ☆ String
- ☆ Large soft sweets (jelly ones work well) – preferably in dark purple and orange
- ☆ Black, white and orange card
- ☆ Pens
- ☆ Skewer

HOW TO MAKE IT:

1. Cut the coloured card into triangles and decorate. Favourite witchy bunting themes include cats, witches' hats, mermaid tails, stars, Fran's face.

2. Pierce little holes in the top of the triangles with the skewer, and thread through the string.

3. Also pierce the sweets with the skewer and thread these too, creating your own design.

4. String it up all over the place. Bite at it whenever you're peckish.

Clutterbucks

'I've never been inside Clutterbucks before,' Lizzie Beast grunted.

Clutterbucks is Ritzy City's most famous secret café, and you need to be a member to get in.

Not long before Tiga and the others arrived, Mrs Clutterbuck had been above the pipes, which is technically illegal. She'd managed to convince NAPA (the National Above the Pipes Association) that it would be a good cultural experience for her. She'd shot out of a drain and made her way into a sweet shop.

'JUST LOOK AT ALL THESE NEW COCKTAIL INGREDIENTS!' she cried when the four of them took their seats at one of Clutterbucks's famous floating tables, only this time, the table was in the behind-the-scenes

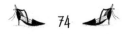

YOU'RE NEVER ALLOWED TO GO IN THERE Clutterbucks kitchen.

'Wow,' Tiga said, spinning around and taking everything in. Machines bubbled over with Clutterbucks cocktails, five-tiered cakes floated past, and busy witches with beaming smiles danced around, adding glitter sprinkles to floating cocktails. 'We should stop by Linden House after this and say hello to Peggy,' Tiga said to Fluffanora. 'Tell her what we've done so far!'

'NO!' Fluffanora screamed, making Tiga jump backwards and into a floating cake. Fluffanora coughed. 'I mean, let's … not do that.'

'Why?' Tiga asked, an eyebrow raised. 'You're being weird.'

'Will you help me make a new Clutterbucks cocktail?' Mrs Clutterbuck interrupted. 'We'll call it the Above the Pipes Potion, or something.'

Tiga giggled. Mrs Clutterbuck was always so cheery, Tiga could hardly imagine what a bunch of humans in a sweet shop would've made of her.

'Fine,' Fran said. 'But we need to interview you about your adventure above the pipes. Your segment for the Witchoween documentary can't just be about these funny things you've brought back from up there.'

'That's all I did, really,' Mrs Clutterbuck said. 'I also watched some very interesting lights that were in charge of the cars.'

'You mean traffic lights?' Tiga asked, an eyebrow raised.

'Is that what they call them?' Mrs Clutterbuck mused. 'Yes, the masters of the cars and trucks.'

'They aren't *the masters* of the cars and tr–' Tiga began, but Fran screamed 'ACTION!' and interrupted her.

All around them, Clutterbucks cocktails in tall glasses burst into life as if on cue and whizzed past, neatly arranging themselves on trays, while Mrs Clutterbuck laid out all the ingredients to make the cocktail.

'PAUSE!' Fran said, clicking her fingers. 'For this one, I'd like to wear all orange.'

'No,' Fluffanora said.

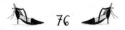
76

'STOP SWEARING!' Fran bellowed.

Fluffanora rolled her eyes. ' "No" isn't a swear word.' She reached into her trunk and pulled out a tiny orange jumpsuit.

Fran wriggled into it. 'AND ACTION, AGAIN!'

'We're here with another Witchoween witch, the wonderful Mrs Clutterbuck, owner of Clutterbucks and creator of the best witchy cocktails in town.

Mrs Clutterbuck has just been above the pipes, where she has sourced some strange human ingredients to make a new cocktail.'

'The Above-the-Pipes Potion,' Mrs Clutterbuck interrupted.

Fran's face strained as she tried not to drop glittery dust out of her skirt in anger. 'No interrupting,' she mumbled out of the corner of her mouth.

'What ingredients did you get?' Tiga asked, picking up a bar of chocolate.

'That's chocolattil,' Mrs Clutterbuck said.

'It's chocolate,' Tiga corrected her.

'Chocotrupy,' Mrs Clutterbuck tried again.

'Cho-co-late,' Tiga tried again.

'Chocnofferin,' Mrs Clutterbuck said, this time into the camera.

'Good enough,' Tiga said with a sigh.

'What we're going to do,' Mrs Clutterbuck said, 'is to blend this chocolatterom with some of those magic bits.'

'Coloured sprinkles,' Tiga corrected her.

'And some cream,' Mrs Clutterbuck added.

'Lovely,' Tiga said, tipping the cream into the cauldron.

'We'll mix it up!' Mrs Clutterbuck said, flicking her finger at the cauldron. 'And then we'll decorate the glasses with these bits of wobbly mystery.'

'Jelly sweets,' Tiga said.

'Oooh,' Fluffanora said. 'May I have a wobbly mystery?'

She grabbed the packet and started munching.

Lizzie Beast cleared her throat loudly. 'Where's the micro cat? Fluffanora?'

'FROGCRUTCHES!' Fran bellowed as the door to Clutterbucks closed. 'IT'S GOT ITS COLLAR OFF AND IS RUNNING AWAY ON ITS LITTLE MICRO LEGS!'

TOAD
MAGAZINE

EXTRA, EXTRA! MAGIC EXTRA CONTENT STRAIGHT FROM OUR SPY! CLUTTERBUCKS AND JUMPSUITS AND WOBBLY MYSTERIES, OH MY!

We've got a juicy update for you today from behind the scenes of the incredibly cool Witchoween documentary.

According to our spy, Fran has been arguing with Fluffanora about whether she can wear an orange jumpsuit. They also visited a **MERMAID MUSEUM** and interviewed Mrs Clutterbuck about smuggling human sweets! Delicious gossip!

Five Things You Didn't Know About Mrs Clutterbuck, by Tiga

1. She didn't pay for the sweets (she only had sinkels), so she technically robbed the place. Human police are searching for her.

2. She first started making Clutterbucks cocktails for her friends when she was seven years old. She had a stall outside her house on Ritzy Avenue and dreamed of opening a secret café, for specially chosen witches.

3. She was bullied at school, and the mean witches would laugh and call her Clutterbucks cocktails stupid.

4. The witches who bullied her are now on a waiting list to get into Clutterbucks. Mrs Clutterbuck hasn't decided whether to let them in or not.

5. She also owns Wigit, the hairdressers' on Lovely Lane, which specialises in fairy beehives and spells that change your hair colour depending on the weather.

How to Make a
Clutterbucks Cocktail

The classic Clutterbucks cocktail, and Tiga's favourite,
the Witching Whirl

WHAT YOU'LL NEED:

- ☆ A tall glass
- ☆ A cool straw
- ☆ Vanilla ice cream
- ☆ Lemonade
- ☆ Edible glitter (or sprinkles)

HOW TO MAKE IT:

1. Add a scoop of ice cream to the glass.
2. Add lemonade (it'll start fizzing – don't let it overflow. If it overflows and spills on the table, we call that a Witching Whirlspill in Clutterbucks. Also delicious, but it tastes more like a table than a drink).

3. Sprinkle on the edible glitter or sprinkles.

4. Add the straw.

5. Put on your witch's hat and enjoy!

8
Brollywood

As the four of them stood outside Clutterbucks sipping what was left of their takeaway cocktails, a piece of perfectly crisp paper landed on top of Fran's beehive.

'Uh-oh,' she said, reading it carefully, her eyeballs bulging. 'WE HAVE A LETTER FROM PATRICIA THE PRODUCER!' She took off, flying in wonky circles around Tiga's head before crash-landing on her nose. 'A LETTER FROM PATRICIA THE PRODUCER!'

'What does it say?' Tiga asked as Lizzie Beast unfolded it from the crumpled mess Fran had left it in on the floor.

'She wants to see us,' Lizzie Beast said gravely. 'Right now.'

'It must be about the *Toad* magazine leak,' Fran said, using her beehive to wipe away terrified tears. 'She hates stuff like that. Once Julie Jumbo Wings told a *Toad* reporter that Crispy was thinking of doing a sequel to her hit film *Toe Pinchers* and they wrote a whole article titled "How to Survive *Toe Pinchers 2*, if Crispy Is Ever Allowed To Make It".'

'What did Patricia the producer do?' Tiga dared to ask.

'People say she cut off Julie Jumbo Wings' toes, and Crispy's too!'

'That's a load of old toad,' Fluffanora said dismissively. 'Anyway, you don't even need toes. You can fly.'

'THEY ARE EXCELLENT FEET DECOR-ATIONS, YOU MONSTER!'

'Well, we're heading that way anyway, we'd better go and see what she wants,' Lizzie Beast said, trudging off towards Brollywood as Tiga and Fluffanora followed.

'Bye,' Fran whispered quietly to her toes before flying off after the others.

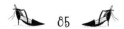

Brollywood was where all the TV shows and films were made, and the pipes that hung above it were particularly drippy. Patricia the producer was in charge of almost everything in Brollywood, and she was responsible for some of the most successful TV shows of all time, including the kids' TV game show *Washy Cat*, and Fran's infamous *Cooking for Tiny People*. She didn't have an office – she had a fake plastic castle.

And it was terrifying.

The last time Tiga had been there was when she and Peggy broke in during Witch Wars to find out who had nominated Tiga for the competition in the first place. Now she was back, and in even more trouble.

'Take a seat, Tiga,' Patricia the producer said coldly. 'You've been here before, haven't you?'

'I can't apologise enough for the breaking and entering, Patricia the producer,' Tiga said, her eyes fixed firmly on her boots.

'So when are you going to cut off our toes?' Fran asked nervously.

'Why would I do that?' Patricia the producer asked.

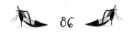

86

'As a punishment for information about *Witch Snitch* being leaked to *Toad* magazine,' Fran prattled on. 'And because that's what you did to Crispy and Julie Jumbo Wings when they leaked information by accident once.'

'What are you talking about?!' Patricia the producer cried. 'I called you here for an update on the documentary – I don't care about *Toad* magazine.'

'Oh good,' Tiga said. 'Because we honestly didn't notice the micro cat.'

Patricia the producer had the strained look of a witch who needed a lie-down. 'And Fran,' she said faintly. 'As far as I'm aware, Crispy and Julie still have all their toes.'

Tiga could hear tiny sniggers behind her.

'I'VE BEEN HAD!' Fran cried, spinning round and pointing a finger at Crispy and Julie Jumbo Wings, who were waving their toes at her and snort-laughing uncontrollably.

Five Things You Didn't Know About Patricia the Producer, by Tiga (for fun)

1. Patricia the producer was once a fairy, but she took a potion to make herself bigger. It worked on everything apart from her ears, which are still fairy-sized.

2. The fake plastic castle that she works in was part of the set of her first ever film – *Easily Melted Castles & Other Quick Battles.*

3. The rest of her family is still fairy-sized, which makes Witchmas dinner difficult (Witchmas is a lot like Christmas only a fat witch with a black beard falls down your chimney rather than Santa with his white one).

4. She has worked on more award-winning films and TV shows than any other witch in the whole of Sinkville history.

5. In Fran's book *Fabulous Me*, she describes Patricia the producer as 'smart, strict, and not someone to leave alone with your toes'.

The Costume Cupboard

Tiga chased Fran as the furious fairy zigzagged between the sets in Brollywood, before coming to an abrupt halt at the Costume Cupboard. In front of the door stood a large witch security guard.

'Is this the cupboard Peggy and I took the wigs from during Witch Wars?' Tiga asked, tapping her toe as she tried to remember.

'No,' Fran said, pointing across the street, just as a witch riding a gigantic fake spider scuttled past. 'You took wigs from the Prop Cupboard. This is the *Costume* Cupboard. LIZZIE BEAST!' she roared. 'START FILMING.'

Fluffanora pulled up next to them, lugging her trunk. 'Is this the place?'

Tiga flicked through her notebook. 'Must be.'

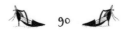

6.   Christy Brunts, coordinator of the Costume Cupboard in Brollywood

'This,' Fran said, smiling into the camera, 'is the Costume Cupboard. The most heavily guarded building in all of Brollywood.'

'WHY IS IT HEAVILY GUARDED?' Fluffanora shouted from behind the camera, winking at Tiga.

'I DON'T KNOW WHY WARDROBE IS TALKING!' Fran screamed. 'Well, the reason it's so heavily guarded is because inside is the last surviving copy of *The Many Faces of Christy Brunts: A Brunts-in-a-Lifetime Spell Book*.'

'I've never heard of it,' Tiga said.

'Exactly,' Fran said. 'Almost every witch has either never been told about it or forgot about it a long, long time ago. And now, the only remaining copy of that spell book is in this very cupboard. And we're going to see it!'

'I'm afraid you'll need permission,' the witch security guard said.

'What's that?' Fran asked, looking confused. 'Is it a type of vegetable?'

'Let them in,' Patricia the producer said, as she floated past with her umbrella. 'I forgot to add them to the list. They're allowed.'

Fran shook her head. 'No, no, Patricia, apparently we can't enter without the permission vegetable.'

'JUST GO IN, FRAN.'

☆⭐☆

The three witches crowded around the giant book, which sat smartly on a stand in the middle of the room, as Fran heaved and huffed and turned the pages. Christy Brunts stood watching them. She was a young witch with curly hair and a huge fabric hairband. She didn't look nearly old enough to have written the ancient spell book they were all poring over.

'It was invented by my great-great-great-great-great-great-great –'

SEVEN MINUTES LATER …

'– great-great-grandmother. There have been many Christy Brunts in our family and I am the latest one. Whoever is given the name Christy Brunts has to do this job, and look after that book.'

'What if you don't want to?' Fluffanora asked.

'WARDROBE!' Fran squealed. 'ZIIIIIP IIIIT!'

'This book,' Christy Brunts said confidently into the camera, 'is *The Many Faces of Christy Brunts: A Brunts-in-a-Lifetime Spell Book* and it saves a fortune in expensive costumes and prosthetic nose costs. All the actors in Brollywood arrive early on set, come to this room and are magically transformed into their character, with the help of secret spells from this very book.'

There was a bang in the corner, and a little witch was transformed into a gigantic cat wearing rubber gloves.

'Hello, Washy Cat!' Fran called over.

'What's *Washy Cat*?' Tiga whispered to Fluffanora.

'It's a kids' TV programme – for little kids. Washy Cat washes up – it's him versus a young witch and they

see who can get through their pile of dirty dishes first. I used to really like it. In retrospect though, it's a load of rubbish.'

'I was once on *Washy Cat*,' Lizzie Beast grunted.

'Did you win?' Tiga asked.

Lizzie Beast shook her head, making the camera shake too. 'No, I broke everything.'

Washy Cat spotted her and cowered.

She looked guiltily at her massive hands. 'Including Washy Cat.'

'The witch who plays Washy Cat is next on your list, Tiga!' Fluffanora said, waving the notebook.

'Now,' Fran said through gritted teeth, 'LIZZIE BEAST, KEEP THE CAMERA STILL. And cut me saying LIZZIE BEAST, KEEP THE CAMERA STILL. What character would you like to be, Tiga?'

'Um …' Tiga said. 'Pardon?'

'For the demonstration Christy Brunts is about to do,' Fran said, smiling into the camera.

'I didn't realise there was, um, going to be one?' Tiga said nervously.

'Well, there is,' Fran snapped. 'Pick a character you'd like to be.'

'A character? I can't really think of –'

'Aaaaaanyone in Sinkville,' Fran pressed, pointing at her own beehive. 'ANYONE.'

Tiga took a seat and rested her chin on her hands, thinking.

'I can't believe it's taking you this long,' Fran huffed, folding her arms. 'ME. *ME*. You probably want to be *MEEEEE*.'

'Oh no, I don't think –' Fluffanora began. But it was too late; Christy Brunts was already chanting the spell.

> *Brunts, Brunts, Brunts, Brunts,*
> *Brunts, Brunts, Brunts, Brunts,*
> *Brunts, Brunts, Brunts, Brunts,*
> *BRUNTS!*

There was a CRACK! The room seemed to get larger. Lizzie Beast began growing at five foot a second.

Fluffanora's dress ballooned. And Fran's hair grew and grew until it looked like the size of a witch's beehive.

Tiga turned and caught a glimpse of her reflection in the window. She was small. She had a beehive. She was … FRAN!

'She's tiny,' Lizzie Beast said, her massive face moving closer. 'And Fran-shaped.'

'TURN ME BACK! TURN ME BACK!' Tiga screamed.

She wobbled in the air – the weird sensation of wings was making her woozy. She could feel them strapped to her back.

'Keep rolling,' she heard Fluffanora whisper to Lizzie Beast. 'We can make a spin-off comedy show out of this stuff.'

'I HEARD THAT!' Tiga roared, her voice irritating and squeaky. 'FAIRIES HAVE VERY SENSITIVE HEARING! Wait a second, *Fran*, that means when you ignore the things I say and claim you didn't hear you're actually *lying*!'

Fran turned and flashed Tiga an innocent look. 'Pardon? I didn't hear you.'

'AAAARGH!' Tiga roared. Now she was a fairy she couldn't seem to control her temper. She could almost feel her blood boiling. 'TURN ME BACK! I DON'T WANT TO BE A SMALL FAIRY! TURN ME BACK, FRAN!'

'You know,' Fran said, taking a seat back on the book. 'I'm slightly offended you're so vehemently against being a fairy. Specifically a *me* fairy.'

Tiga felt a hissing noise in her ears. Smoke was coming out of them!

'Oh dear,' Fluffanora said, diving for the book. 'She's going to pop.'

> *REVERSE Brunts, REVERSE Brunts,*
> *REVERSE Brunts, REVERSE Brunts,*
> *REVERSE Brunts, REVERSE Brunts,*
> *REVERSE Brunts, REVERSE Brunts,*
> *REVERSE Brunts, REVERSE Brunts,*
> *REVERSE Brunts, REVERSE Brunts,*
> *REVERSE BRUNTS!*

Five Things You Didn't Know About Christy Brunts, by Tiga

1. Christy Brunts isn't magic, because the name Christy Brunts was cursed over three hundred years ago. Christy Brunts can only be magic when using the Christy Brunts book.

2. Christy Brunts once tried to change her name when she heard a four-year-old called Anna changed her name successfully to Fluffanora, but the Sinkville Name Office said Queen Wendybottle Brunts was not an acceptable name.

3. She also tried to change her name to Franolima.

4. And Bungle.

5. And Toaster. None were accepted.

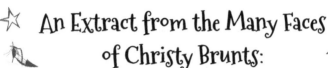

An Extract from the Many Faces of Christy Brunts:

A Brunts-in-a-Lifetime Spell Book

COSTUMES & SPELLS:

HOW TO BE TIGA, FLUFFANORA, ETC.

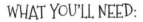

WHAT YOU'LL NEED:

- ☆ The ability to say 'Brunts'
- ☆ And the following items, depending on who you want to be:

FLUFFANORA

1. A long skirt.
2. To make it puffy, wear an underskirt underneath.
3. A glamorous hat – you can decorate it yourself, like Fluffanora. She likes to wrap beaded necklaces around her hat. You can also glue white feathers to it for special occasions.

4. Some cool shoes and spotted or striped tights.
5. Dark sunglasses for when you want to walk down the street without one of the *Toad* reporters spotting you.
6. Bracelets – Fluffanora likes to mix and match bracelets, especially ones she's beaded herself.

TIGA

1. A spotted skirt.
2. Striped tights.
3. Silver braces (these are optional, but they're Tiga's favourite thing in her wardrobe at the moment).
4. A striped top with long sleeves.
5. A glamorous black hat.
6. A slug with a beehive of hair.
7. Some really cool boots. Tiga likes to change the laces, mixing and matching different colours so the left bootlace clashes with the right bootlace. Very cool.

LIZZIE BEAST

1. A really long wig (unless you've been growing your hair for a really long time).
2. A cool grey hat.
3. A long simple grey skirt (school skirts work really well).
4. Flat sandals.
5. Striped tights.
6. Lizzie Beast really likes brooches – cool vintage ones she borrows from her grandmother. She likes to pin them to her jumper.
7. Add a choker – she likes to wear these on special occasions.

FRAN

1. Wings.
2. Glittery dust.
3. A sparkly skirt.
4. A beehive hairstyle.
5. A star hairband.
6. Excellent shoes.

WASHY CAT

1. Washing-up gloves.
2. Whiskers (these can be drawn on).
3. Cat ears.
4. Hairy cat arms.
5. A boiler suit or dungarees, and a black T-shirt.

Washy Cat

'Washy Cat,' Fran tried. 'Washy Cat?'

Pip Glow, the witch who played Washy Cat, was slowly edging towards the door.

'We just want to do a quick bit of filming with you for our Witchoween documentary,' Fran said, flying closer.

'STAY AWAY!' Pip Glow shouted from inside the Washy Cat costume, pointing at Lizzie Beast and falling out of the door.

Tiga peeked outside just in time to see her grab a broom and fly off, wobbling in her Washy Cat costume and shedding hair as she went.

'I guess we won't be interviewing Washy Cat,' Fran said, glaring at Lizzie Beast.

Five Things You Didn't Know About Pip Glow, by Tiga

1. Pip Glow has played Washy Cat for longer than any other witch actress, ever.

2. Over thirty thousand young witches write to Washy Cat every year and she replies to all of them.

3. She refuses to talk about the episode of *Washy Cat* featuring a five-year-old Lizzie Beast. The episode is occasionally shown on Fairy 5, as a horror film.

4. In Pip Glow's memoirs, called *Washing Away the Witch*, she says the Washy Cat costume weighs the same as four thousand overweight cats.

5. She volunteers at Sinkville's cat hospital in the towers once a month.

Toad Magazine

'Ready?' Lizzie Beast asked.

Fran rubbed her teeth and smiled into the camera. 'Only if you're not going to say three, two, one and go again, Lizzie Beast.'

'*WITCH SNITCH!* Behind the scenes at *Toad* magazine with Darcy Dream, TAKE ONE!' Lizzie Beast shouted.

'And here we find ourselves outside the very exclusive offices of fashion and gossip magazine *Toad*,' Fran oozed. 'No one is allowed in, apart from the select witches who work here. But today, for the first time, we have been granted unprecedented access! We'll see how a *Toad* magazine is put together, find out more about the witches behind it and lots more! So follow me as I go inside this *Toad*.' She flew to the door and smacked into it.

'HELLO! IT'S LOCKED!'

'I think you just have to turn the handle,' Tiga said quietly.

'Handles that turn,' Fran scoffed. 'That is *so* above the pipes. You'd think a magazine as forward-thinking as *Toad* would have bewitched doors.'

Inside, *Toad* magazine's office was slick. A jet-black catwalk-style carpet led to the reception desk, where a young witch sat applying silver lipstick.

'Name,' she said without looking away from her mirror.

'Tiga,' Tiga said. 'We're filming the Witchoween documentary. We're here to see Darcy Dream.'

'Fifth floor,' the witch said, pouting in the mirror.

Tiga looked around. There didn't seem to be any stairs, or a lift.

'How do we get to the fifth fl–?'

'Levitation,' the witch said. 'It's a requirement when working here. If you can't levitate ten floors, then you can't work here.'

Fluffanora stepped forward. 'Fine, we'll levitate. But can someone please carry my trunk for me?'

The witch looked up, her eyes wide. 'Fluffanora Brew!' she cried. 'Oh, I didn't realise *you* were part of the documentary too.' She levitated in the air and flicked her finger. 'Let me take that trunk for you.'

And up they went. The receptionist, Fluffanora and the gigantic trunk. Tiga tried to mumble the levitation spell but barely rose off the ground before falling back down again. She wasn't good under pressure.

'Allow me,' Fran said through gritted teeth, clearly annoyed that Fluffanora was getting all the attention. And with that, Tiga and Lizzie Beast rose up high in a big puff of glittery dust to the fifth floor. They passed layers of witches floating about on floors crammed with clothes and boards covered in magazine pages – all laid out for the next issue.

'The fifth floor,' Fran shouted down to Lizzie Beast, who was floating slightly slower than the rest of them due to the weight of the camera, 'IS WHERE DARCY DREAM'S OFFICE IS. SHE'S THE EDITOR AND

DOES A VERY GOOD JOB THAT ONLY I COULD DO BETTER.'

'Hello, Fran,' Darcy Dream said, ushering them into a pristine white office.

'Set up over there, Lizzie Beast,' Fran said, pointing to the corner of the room.

'I love your hair,' Darcy Dream said. She was wearing a silver polo neck with an orange strappy dress over it and strings and strings of jam-red beads around her neck.

'Why, thank you. I've had this beehive since I was born,' Fran said. 'All of it.'

'Actually I meant her,' Darcy Dream said, pointing at Lizzie Beast.

Fran's beehive flopped.

Over in the corner of the room, Fluffanora pulled some skirts from the trunk and held them up to Tiga. 'You need to look fashionable for this section of the documentary.'

'I'm always fashionable!' Tiga cried.

'You need to be high fashion,' Fluffanora said.

'What does that even mean?' Tiga asked.

'It means wearing an outfit so unusual that people have no idea where you got it from. Plus it's really weird in a cool way.'

'Like you!' Tiga said.

'Funny,' Fluffanora said as she threw the first skirt over her shoulder.

'I'm glad you're here. And Lizzie Beast. I would've gone completely mad on my own with Fran,' Tiga said.

'Obviously.' Fluffanora flicked her finger and floated a line of tops in front of Tiga. 'She's a tiny menace.'

'I wish Peggy was here,' Tiga said. 'I wonder what she's doing.'

'She's doing nothing,' Fluffanora said quickly. 'Absolutely NOTHING. Nothing.'

'Nothing?' Tiga said, confused. 'But she's the Top Witch, she's doing *something*.'

'But it's nothing secret or anything,' Fluffanora said, flicking her finger again and changing Tiga's clothes. She was in an electric-blue ankle-length skirt and fluffy white jumper with a chunky parrot charm necklace.

'You're being weird,' Tiga said. She looked at her feet, which Fluffanora had clad in some sparkling purple shoes. 'Every time I bring up Peggy, you –'

'Sssh,' Fluffanora said. 'I'm trying to decide if those shoes are right for that outfit.'

'You're being weird,' Tiga said again, crossing her arms.

'WARDROBE!' Fran roared. 'I THINK WE CAN MAKE MY HAIR RED FOR THIS BIT, WHICH MEANS THE LITTLE STAR CHARM ACCESSORIES WILL CLASH NOW!'

'Better go,' Fluffanora said, darting across the room as quickly as she could.

It wasn't like her to bend easily to Fran's demands, Tiga thought. She was acting very suspiciously …

'THIS,' Fran boomed, shattering Tiga's thoughts, 'is Darcy Dream, and she's in an editorial meeting. In the editorial meeting, the *Toad* team discuss what they are going to put in the next issue of the magazine and Darcy Dream gets to say YES! NO! HORRIBLE RUBBISH WITCHES! I LIKE STRIPES! And things like that.'

'Let's make it all about hair,' Darcy Dream said. 'Her hair.' She pointed to Lizzie Beast behind the camera.

'I know the medium of film isn't exactly your area,' Fran whispered to her, 'but you're really not meant to point into the camera.'

Darcy Dream glared at her.

'I'll let it go this once,' Fran said, her nose in the air. 'You are, after all, an amateur.'

'NEXT UP IS THE FASHION CUPBOARD!' Fran roared. 'Created by Darcy Dream when she founded *Toad* magazine ages ago.'

'And it grows bigger each year,' Darcy Dream said, pointing into the camera again, this time, Tiga suspected, just to annoy Fran.

'Finger,' Fran said with a sigh.

Tiga marched through the cupboard. The cupboard was hardly a cupboard at all – it was a gigantic room, even bigger than the first floor of Brew's. Trendy witches levitated up high to rails, pulling clothes out and discussing them in hushed whispers.

'I could see you working somewhere like this,' Tiga said to Fluffanora.

'I'm going to *design* the clothes,' Fluffanora said. 'One day witches will be picking my clothes from these racks.'

'It's Fluffanora,' a levitating witch whispered.

'Oh, cute – look, she's got a notebook covered in *Toad* magazine clippings!' said another.

Tiga saw Fluffanora's cheeks flush purple.

'I bet the micro cat is in here,' Fran whispered to

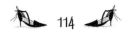

Tiga. 'I wonder where its office is … We can't let it follow us out when we leave. We can't have any more leaks.'

Tiga nodded. 'I'll look out for it.'

Fran hovered next to a witch with pink wooden glasses, slicked-back hair and silky black overalls.

'How do you know which clothes to pick?' Fran asked, sounding genuinely fascinated.

The witch stared intently into the camera. 'Either we pick good stuff. Or new stuff.'

'Right,' Fran said. 'That makes sense. And what is the new cool thing this week?'

The witch stared intently into the camera. 'Either shoes with mushrooms printed on them or yellow everything.'

'Yeah, this stuff isn't that good,' Fran said, pulling at a feathered black dress. 'Plus it's all too big for me. That's enough of this section, Lizzie Beast. AND CUT!'

☆彡☆

Toad's art department was their final stop with Darcy Dream. Tiga watched with amazement as witches floated around amongst all the pieces of the unfinished

Toad magazine. The art director, Melly Marker, was putting some finishing touches to the latest issue's cover – it featured the word TOAD covered in what looked a lot like Lizzie Beast's hair.

'Your hair is famous,' Fluffanora said, nudging Lizzie Beast.

'Yes, well,' Fran mumbled jealously. 'For one week. My hair has been famous for years.'

Melly Marker turned to one of the assistants and shouted, 'I think it needs to be yellow. Everything in fashion is yellow this week. Black hair, yellow for the *Toad* title.'

The witch assistant nodded, and just like that, the *Toad* title was yellow.

Melly Marker put her hands on her hips and stared intently at the cover.

'What's she doing?' Fran whispered to Tiga.

Tiga shrugged. 'I think she might be trying to decide if she likes it.'

'Can we make the yellow glow?' Melly Marker asked. 'I need it to glow.'

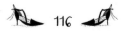

One by one, the letters began to glow, in various shades of yellow.

'Let's go with vibrant sun yellow, definitely not that sand colour,' Darcy Dream said. 'Get it printed.'

'And that,' Fran said, turning to the camera, 'is Darcy Dream. And this week her magazine is a glowing yellow beacon in this horrible snow-capped cold place full of evil witches that is known as Pearl Peak.'

The entire office fell silent. Every witch in the room stared.

'What?' Fran said with a dismissive shrug. 'Pearl Peak is where the evil witches live. Everyone knows that.'

Tiga tried not to smile as everyone got back to work.

'You know,' Fluffanora said. 'You could make some fabulous party invites that look like *Toad* magazine.'

'Quick,' Fran hissed. 'We need to leave now. I've got the micro cat – stashed in my beehive.'

Five Things You Didn't Know About Darcy Dream, by Tiga

1. Her real name is Darcy Dragpit, but when she became editor of *Toad* magazine she changed it to Dream, to sound more friendly.

2. Before she was editor, she wrote a column for *Toad* called SHOETASTROPHES, about shoes that she decided were catastrophes.

3. She washes her hair with Cackleoo, the most expensive witch shampoo, containing actual bottled cackles from witches with great hair.

4. An interviewer once asked her what she thought of fashion above the pipes. She said, 'Not enough hats.'

5. Her sister, Margot Dragpit, runs a small boutique in Pearl Peak called Dragpit's Dresses. It is known for selling only black clothing, and illegal spells.

How to Make Perfect Party Invites, *Toad Magazine-Style*

WHAT YOU'LL NEED:

- ☆ Coloured card
- ☆ Scissors
- ☆ An envelope
- ☆ Colouring pens
- ☆ Possibly a picture of your face

HOW TO MAKE THEM:

1. Cut a piece of card to invite size and fold in half.

2. Cut two parallel slits on the folded side of the card.

3. Fold up the tab and crease it.

4. Open up the card and pop the tab so it's popped up on the inside of the card.

5. Design the inside of the card, writing all the important information: who you're inviting,

where it is, explain there will be cake and you really like presents (or don't. Apparently this is OK if you're a witch, but not as OK if you're a human).

6. It's also tradition to make up a secret code to get into your party. Previous examples from Melinda Zing's Witchoween parties include 'wuddleup', 'TOES' and 'ni emoc nac uoy sey', which is 'yes you can come in' backwards.

7. Next, get a cool picture, or a picture of your face, and attach it to the popped-up tab with some glue. Now whoever opens the card will be greeted with a pop-up picture of your face!*

*This party invitation idea was brought to you by Fran, who really likes her face.

The Best Bedroom in Pearl Peak

Tiga wasn't looking forward to the next stop.

The streets of Pearl Peak were quiet – witches clad in black slipped down side streets like they were up to no good. The towering grand buildings, all shiny and black, were framed by the gigantic snow-tipped mountain that loomed large in the distance.

Fran skidded to a halt outside No. 10 Pearl Peak Place and slotted neatly through the large iron gates, which were covered in an assorted animal hoof pattern, studded with black diamonds.

Fluffanora sighed as she pushed the gate open. 'Here we go …'

'This is Fluffy. My octopus,' Aggie Hoof said into the camera. A gigantic octopus with diamond-studded tentacles bobbed up and down in a fifty-foot fish tank. Purple lights illuminated him from every angle.

'Why is it called *Fluffy*?' Fluffanora asked. 'It's not fluffy.'

'Because that's his name,' Aggie Hoof said defensively. 'Your name has Fluff in it and *you're* not fluffy.'

'Fair point,' Fluffanora said with a shrug.

'And, Aggie Hoof,' Fran said, spinning in the air and smiling into the camera. 'What's your favourite part of your bedroom?'

'Me when I'm standing in it,' Aggie Hoff answered.

Tiga scanned the room. Aside from the gigantic illuminated fish tank, there was a grand four-poster bed with a den on top of it, stacked with old *Toad* magazines. A door to the left led into a gigantic wardrobe – it appeared to be never-ending, stretching off into the distance. And a little witch-shaped robot stood beside it.

'What does the robot do?' Tiga asked.

'It shows me what clothes are in my wardrobe so I

don't need to try them on,' Aggie Hoof said. 'It's called a DressMe, and I'm the only one who owns one.'

Tiga walked over to the robot.

'Tell it what you'd like to wear,' Aggie Hoof said.

'Um,' Tiga began. 'I'd like … a nice cloak or coat?'

The robot raised its arms and with a magic CRACK, Tiga looked down to see a hologram of a beautiful lace cape now covering her. To her right was a little digital map of where to find it in the huge maze of a wardrobe.

'Ask what it thinks would go best with the cloak. It's programmed with my fashion sense.'

'What would go with the cloak?' Tiga asked.

There was another CRACK, and Tiga looked down to see some sparkly gold platform shoes and a pair of yellow trousers.

'Yellow is really in at the moment,' Aggie Hoof said knowingly.

'They were just saying that at *Toad*,' Fran said, sounding impressed.

'I know,' Aggie Hoof said, trotting over to her desk and lifting the head off of a cat ornament. Inside was a

button. When she pressed it, a huge image of the *Toad* fashion cupboard appeared on the wall. 'I bugged their offices when I was four.'

'And what's behind this door?' Fran asked, trying to slide a particularly shiny black door open.

'That's my restaurant,' Aggie Hoof said, flicking her finger and sending the door crashing open.

Tiga and Fluffanora gasped.

Lizzie Beast dropped her camera and hastily picked it back up again. Inside was a grand restaurant with a single table perched in the middle. A slick black tablecloth covered it, and on it, plate upon plate of delicious food was piled high. There was a huge fountain spitting out a strange black gooey liquid that smelled a lot like caramel. Trays of what looked like jam-covered pizzas sat on one side, next to some black hamburgers with jelly-like jam slices piled inside. Little witch waitresses ran around frantically, as if they were serving a hundred witches.

'It serves all my favourite foods,' Aggie Hoof boasted. 'And I have *millions* of favourite foods.'

'Is that where you eat?' Fluffanora asked. 'All alone?'

'Yes,' Aggie Hoof said proudly. 'Sometimes my best friend, Fel-Fel, eats there with me too. But she doesn't like restaurants. She says they smell too much of other people's food.'

Tiga's tummy rumbled.

Aggie Hoof stared at her sternly. 'Oh go on,' she said with a grin, as Tiga dived for the table.

☆🔭☆

'And the artwork you have in this place is *spectacular*,' Fran said after they'd finished dinner. Tiga rubbed her full tummy. The black burgers with jelly slice fillings were her favourite.

Fran pointed at a painting of two witches flying past the moon. 'I especially enjoy that painting, though it needs a fairy.'

'Oh,' Aggie Hoof said, taking a seat on her bed. 'That's not a painting. It's a portal.'

'A portal,' Tiga said, suddenly excited. 'Where does it lead?'

'Does it lead to another wardrobe?' Fluffanora asked, sounding bored.

'No!' Aggie Hoof said, leaping from the bed and diving through the painting.

The four of them stood and stared at each other. Fran rubbed her hands together and sighed. 'Right, who dares to go after her?'

Five Things You Didn't Know About Aggie Hoof, by Tiga

1. Aggie Hoof won an award when she was three years old for the witch who could scream the alphabet the fastest. The award is called the AaaarghBCD.

2. She has been sneaking up the pipes for the past three years and has a human friend called Kelly.

3. She once had a cat called Lumpy, but Lumpy ran away.

4. She only wears socks made by Frogstockings, which have a small shop just off Bubble Beach in the Cauldron Islands.

5. She can play the wums (witch-style drums) better than any witch in Sinkville and regularly performs in the orchestra at the Ritzytwig theatre.

13

Sleepover at Fel-Fel's

Tiga could feel her feet in her face as she tumbled through the painting and down what felt like a laundry chute.

'ARE WE GOING TO DIE?' she heard Lizzie Beast shout, followed by Fran tutting.

'Lizzie Beast, that is a ridiculous question. *Everything* dies eventually.'

'SO, YES,' Lizzie Beast acknowledged. 'BUT RIGHT NOW, I MEAN?'

Tiga crashed through something that made a ripping sound and landed with a thud on a fluffy black carpet.

Fran came tumbling out after her, followed by Fluffanora, who landed on top of her, then Lizzie Beast, who landed on top of *her*, and finally, the trunk – which they all scattered to avoid.

'Oh great. You're one Peggy from being the full set,' came a voice.

Tiga got to her feet and dusted off her skirt.

'THE PORTAL LEADS TO MY BEST FRIEND FEL-FEL'S BEDROOM!' Aggie Hoof cheered, jumping up and down excitedly.

'Welcome,' Felicity Bat said grumpily. She was wearing bat-patterned pyjamas and a black hairnet. She spotted Tiga staring at it and ripped it from her head, quickly hiding it behind her back. 'Can you please explain why you're in my bedroom?'

'They asked where the portal leads to, Fel-Fel,' Aggie Hoof explained.

Felicity Bat rolled her eyes. 'Well, now you know, so you can leave me in peace. I have a lot of Co-Top Witch homework to do, so if you don't mind.'

Aggie Hoof cuddled her arm.

'*Ugh*,' Felicity Bat groaned, shaking her off. 'You're so annoying.'

'If you find her so annoying, why do you have a portal that connects her bedroom to yours?' Fluffanora asked.

'Because it's a really good spell and I still don't know how she did it,' Felicity Bat hissed. 'And that's fascinating to me.'

'I don't even know how I did it!' Aggie Hoof laughed as she skipped around the room. 'Sometimes I just have magic accidents and they work out really well! I think it's because I'm rich.'

'I think she paid someone to install it,' Felicity Bat

whispered to Tiga. 'It's too good a spell not to be professional.'

'I KNOW!' Fran said, buzzing between them. 'Let's sleep here tonight! It's getting late.'

Felicity Bat levitated over to the painting portal, which on her side of the wall featured a Silver Rats band poster. She sneezed loudly and wiped her nose on her sleeve. 'You've had your fun. Now you need to leave.'

Tiga made her way over to the impressive bookcase that lined the wall.

'What are the books about?' Fran asked.

'Lots of things,' Felicity Bat said impatiently. 'Sink-ville history mostly.'

'And this?' Fran asked.

'That's my wardrobe,' Felicity Bat said, pointing at the normal-sized wardrobe in the corner.

Tiga opened it. It contained five identical dresses and hats.

'Where's all the magic stuff?' Fran asked.

Felicity Bat leaned back in her seat. 'I'm the magic part.'

 133

'This is the most normal, above-the-pipes-style bedroom I've ever seen!' Tiga said, jumping on the bed. It bounced like a normal above-the-pipes bed. It didn't float or ask how your day was like the one at Tiga's house in Silver City. It was covered in cuddly toy spiders of varying sizes.

'What?' Felicity Bat said defensively. 'It's OK to still have toys.'

'I know,' Tiga said. 'I just didn't think you of all people would have *so many*.'

'They are collectors' items, made by Wartwell & Witch. Not *just* toys; they'll be worth millions of sinkels one day.'

'Who are you interviewing next?' Aggie Hoof asked. 'Bet they aren't nearly as good as me.'

Tiga flicked open her notebook. 'Next is Idabelle Bat at the First Witch Who Landed in Sinkville historical site, just outside Pearl Peak.'

Felicity Bat groaned.

Everyone turned to look at her.

'Is that a problem?' Tiga asked.

'That's my big sister,' Felicity Bat said, sticking her nose in the air and levitating across the room.

'Your *sister*?' Tiga said. 'But you've never mentioned you have a sister.'

'On purpose,' Felicity Bat said.

'Is she like you?' Fluffanora asked, suddenly fascinated.

Aggie Hoof mouthed 'no' behind Felicity Bat and shook her head.

'We're quite different,' Felicity Bat said, straightening up her toy spiders. 'She's … how best to put this –'

'She's REALLY cool!' Aggie Hoof interrupted. 'But she *is* mean like you, Fel-Fel.'

'She doesn't even like working there,' Felicity Bat huffed. 'She only does it for the extra sinkels on weekends. I can't believe she's wormed her way into the Witchoween documentary – she hardly knows anything about Sinkville history.' She levitated hastily across the room and pulled a book from the shelves. *The Big Splat*. She sneezed loudly. 'I'm coming with you, to make sure everything that is said on camera is historically accurate. I won't have some food presenter for Fairy 5, my big sister and *Tiga* of all people butchering our glorious history.'

Fran stuck her nose in the air. 'Fine, come along if you must.'

Felicity Bat sneezed again.

'Have you got a cold?' Tiga asked.

'No,' Felicity Bat said. 'I think I'm allergic to you.'

'It's probably the micro cat,' Lizzie Beast grunted.

'There's a micro cat in here?!' Felicity Bat squealed. 'I'm highly allergic!'

'It's probably gone now,' Fluffanora said. 'It's always trying to escape.' She flicked her finger and Felicity Bat's bed got fatter – big enough to fit all of them.

Aggie Hoof rubbed her hands together excitedly. 'I've never been to a sleepover with more than Felicity Bat! This must be what it feels like to have OTHER FRIENDS. I like it.'

Fran yawned and made a beeline for Felicity Bat's bed.

'NO!' Felicity Bat cried, but it was too late. Fran already had her eye mask on.

Five Things You Didn't Know About Felicity Bat, by Tiga (for fun)

1. She has a big sister called Idabelle, who was voted Most Popular Teenage Witch at Pearl Peak Academy eight years in a row.

2. She can recite the full history of Sinkville from the day the first witch landed off by heart and in forty-five minutes.

3. She sends her evil grandmother, Celia Crayfish, packages of treats from Cakes, Pies and That's About It Really, every month (Celia Crayfish is currently working in a cheese factory above the pipes as punishment for trying to seize power in Sinkville from the current Top Witch, Peggy Pigwiggle).

4. She brushes her teeth with SlimeTime, an ancient toothpaste that is now only sold at the Pearl Peak Pharmacy.

5. She has smiled twice. Both times she has denied it.

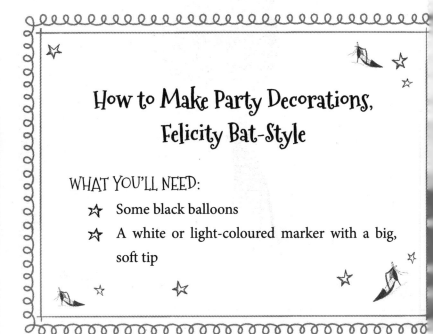

How to Make Party Decorations, Felicity Bat-Style

WHAT YOU'LL NEED:

- ★ Some black balloons
- ★ A white or light-coloured marker with a big, soft tip

HOW TO MAKE THEM:

1. Blow up the balloons.
2. Draw Felicity Bat-style grumpy faces on them.
3. Tie them in a bunch and place them at the entrance to your Witchoween party as a talking point.

The Infamous Idabelle Bat

'Just think,' Fluffanora said. 'If we had known Felicity Bat was allergic to micro cats, we could've just got a micro cat to follow her around during the Witch Wars competition, making her sneeze until she was too busy sneezing to be an evil cheat.'

Felicity Bat rolled her eyes and levitated higher. 'It's just over here.'

In the distance, Tiga could see the tiny eye-blinding lights from the shiny fairy caravan park, and the rooftops of Ritzy City in the distance.

'Where's your trunk?' Tiga asked Fluffanora.

Fluffanora strode on up the hill. 'Lizzie Beast is taking care of it!'

Tiga looked around to see Lizzie Beast sweating

profusely. 'Taking. Care. Of. It,' she wheezed as she balanced the trunk on her back and cradled the camera in her arms. 'TAKING CARE OF IT!'

Felicity Bat stopped dead in her tracks, her boots making a clanging sound as they connected with the rocky mountain. 'There she is,' she muttered.

Tiga squinted into the distance. Up ahead on the hill, making small rocks magically collide in the air, was a teenage witch in a puffy black dress and mud-stained boots. Her hair was just like Felicity Bat's before she'd cut it short. It was like looking at Felicity Bat in ten years' time. A little further up the hill was a tiny ticket booth; a stream of unwanted tickets had unfurled from the hatch and was billowing in the wind.

'TOAD CHOPS!' Idabelle cackled when she saw them approaching.

'Toad chops is what my sister calls me,' Felicity Bat informed them, before anyone had a chance to ask. 'It's an insult that works on multiple levels – it is demeaning in general, plus the use of the word toad also implies that I like *Toad* magazine.'

'SHE LOVES *TOAD* MAGAZINE!' Idabelle shouted over.

'I hate *Toad* magazine,' Felicity Bat insisted.

Her sister levitated above her. 'Seriously, Felicity, it's not even an insult.'

'These are my friends – they're here to interview you for the Witchoween documentary,' Felicity Bat said coldly.

Idabelle bowed. She had the same intense stare as Felicity Bat, and Tiga felt instantly intimidated by her.

'Why is that one practically cowering?' Idabelle asked, pointing at Tiga. 'What's she thinking?'

Tiga looked in horror at Felicity Bat – who could mind read! She desperately tried to think nice thoughts, not thoughts about how scared she was of Idabelle.

'She's thinking,' Felicity Bat began.

Tiga could feel her face turning purple. NOTHING WAS SAFE AROUND FELICITY BAT! Tiga wanted to melt into a big gloop of mouldy jam and slop down the hill.

'She would like to do a re-enactment of the first

witch who landed in Sinkville for the documentary, with you describing it,' Felicity Bat finished.

Idabelle eyed Tiga suspiciously.

'See,' Felicity Bat said mockingly to Tiga. 'Nothing is safe around Felicity Bat!'

Tiga smiled and mouthed 'thank you'.

The re-enactment of the first witch who landed in Sinkville was not going to be easy, Tiga realised. Mostly because Felicity Bat was a stickler for detail. And Fran was keen to somehow incorporate glitter.

'WE CAN'T HAVE GLITTER, BECAUSE GLITTER WASN'T A PART OF WHAT HAP-PENED,' Felicity Bat said sternly.

Fran shot some glitter in protest. 'IT PROBABLY WAS. Glitter is in almost everything.'

Felicity Bat slammed her book shut. 'It's not.'

Tiga made her way over to the witch-shaped hole in the ground. She had landed in a perfect star shape. Around the hole was a glittery rope with various rickety

143

warning signs attached. WARNING! NO FALLING! and NO LOOKING AT THIS HOLE IN THE GROUND WITHOUT A PREPAID TICKET, 100 SINKELS.

'Well, let's get started,' Felicity Bat said. 'I haven't got all day.'

Idabelle flicked her finger and tore a line of tickets from the booth behind them. She handed them to Felicity and hovered silently beside her, a mean grin smacked on her face.

'Who's going to be the witch in the re-enactment?' Tiga asked. 'The witch who … falls from up there.'

They all looked up.

'I'm too small to play a witch,' Fran said quickly.

'I'm busy in Wardrobe,' Fluffanora said, trying to squeeze into her trunk.

'I … could do it,' Tiga said quietly.

'Rubbish,' Fran said with a snort. 'You're the *co-presenter*. Also, I don't want you to die.'

Felicity Bat inspected her nails causally. 'I would do it, but I need to make sure everything looks right and is factually accurate from the ground.'

Idabelle inspected the ends of one of her plaits. 'I'm Idabelle.'

'What do you *mean*, "I'm Idabelle"?' Felicity Bat said.

'I'm Idabelle, so I'm too cool to do it.'

Felicity Bat rolled her eyes, while the rest of them turned slowly towards Lizzie Beast. Fluffanora's trunk opened and she looked too.

'That means there's only …' Fran tailed off.

Lizzie Beast put the camera down.

'Well, she can't do it!' Tiga cried. 'Lizzie Beast is the camera witch! The most important person here!'

Fran tapped her chin and flew back and forth. 'Well, it's between Felicity Bat and Lizzie Beast. I know! Why don't you lie down next to the hole and see which one fits better.'

They both looked at each other before flopping down next to the hole. Felicity Bat appeared tiny and weedy next to the almighty pit of a hole. But Lizzie Beast fitted perfectly.

'But the camera,' Tiga protested.

'It's all right,' Lizzie Beast said with a smile. 'I can teach you how to use it in two seconds.'

'Stop speaking, I'm trying to get you out of this,' Tiga whispered.

'Look,' Idabelle said sternly. 'We're going to be here all day if we don't decide soon. How about Lizzie Beast does it and Toad Chops will make sure, with her advanced and expert spells, that Lizzie Beast hovers right before she hits the hole, and then we'll CUT! And it will look dramatic and perfect.'

Fran clapped loudly. 'Oh, bravo!'

Felicity Bat flipped her book open again. 'Now, according to this, the first witch who landed in Sinkville came from pipe 997 on West 51st row of pipes.' She looked up. 'So it's … that one.'

Tiga took her position behind the camera. Fluffanora sat in her trunk, sipping Clutterbucks and watching the action unfold, like she was in a box seat at the Ritzytwig Theatre.

'We should probably be in costume,' Fran said, as with a single wrinkle of the nose and forceful BOOM, all of them were suddenly in old black cloaks and frilly bonnets.

'Oi!' Fluffanora cried from the hatch. 'I'm in charge of Wardrobe.'

'Tell it to the nose,' Fran said, tapping hers proudly.

Fluffanora grumpily closed the hatch. Tiga watched as the trunk wriggled. Clearly Fluffanora was marching down the corridor inside to get a better outfit.

Felicity Bat flicked her finger and Lizzie Beast began to rise higher and higher until she was nothing more than a speck in the air, a Fran-sized blob below a wall of dripping pipes.

Fran rubbed her hands together with glee.

'It was a windy day,' Idabelle said sinisterly into the camera, wiggling her nose to magic up some extra wind. Tiga looked up and saw Lizzie Beast being swept to the left and smacking into a pipe.

'I'M FINE!' she called down to them.

'And Sinkville,' Idabelle said, lowering her voice to a whisper, 'was *empty*. But then something happened that changed the course of witch history for ever, although how true it is we don't know.'

'WE DO KNOW AND IT'S TRUE,' Felicity Bat

interjected, not taking her eyes off Lizzie Beast, who was now hovering just inside pipe 997.

'What we do know for sure,' Idabelle said, gliding over to the hole, 'is that this here is where –' She paused for dramatic effect. 'THE FIRST WITCH LANDED IN SINKVILLE!'

Tiga swung the camera up to the pipe, and watched, gripping the camera fiercely as Lizzie Beast came somersaulting down, skirt over her head. Tiga nervously looked to Felicity Bat, who seemed completely in control of the situation.

'Remember,' Tiga whispered. 'Stop her before she hits the hole and I'll cut the camera.'

Felicity Bat nodded, which only served to speed Lizzie Beast's fall.

'The witch fell from the pipe!' Idabelle was having to commentate more quickly. 'From the world above! With incredible speed!'

Tiga caught a glimpse of something darting across the ground, past Felicity Bat and towards the hole. She frantically scanned the area, but couldn't catch sight of it.

'Tiga, keep the camera on Lizzie Beast,' Fran hissed.

Tiga peered through the lens. Lizzie Beast was close now, just two more seconds, and then –

ACHOOOOOOO!

There was an almighty crunch! A dusty cloud of soil and stones burst from the hole, completely covering them.

Tiga coughed as the dust cleared. Felicity Bat was angrily wiping her runny nose.

'The micro cat,' Tiga said. 'I saw it darting past!'

'That stupid micro cat! I told you to keep it away from me!' Felicity Bat roared. 'I sneezed and broke the spell!'

Fran turned to Tiga. 'Tiga, why were you not looking after the micro cat?'

'Because no one asked me to!' Tiga said, racing over to where Felicity Bat was hovering by the hole. 'I can hardly *see* the micro cat! How could I possibly look after it?'

'Grizzly Feast is gone,' Idabelle announced flatly.

'It's Lizzie Beast,' Felicity Bat corrected her.

'DEAD?!' Tiga cried.

'No,' Idabelle said, dusting off her skirt. 'She's gone to wherever this shortcut leads.'

'It's a shortcut?' Tiga asked.

'Obviously,' Felicity Bat said. 'Do you know nothing about Sinkville history? The witch who landed here also invented shortcuts. Holes in the ground around Sinkville that link with one of the towers in The Towers.'

Fran began whistling loudly for the micro cat. She stopped near the hole and picked up a tiny lead. 'Uh-oh,' she said, peering into the hole. 'I think the micro cat might've been under Lizzie Beast. Serves it right for running away, really.'

'Well, we need to go to the towers and find out where she's gone to,' Tiga said.

'There's an easy way to find out where she's gone,' Idabelle said with a sinister smile.

And before Tiga could reply, she felt the unmistakeable shove of magic as she tumbled head first into the hole.

Five Things You Didn't Know About Idabelle Bat, by Tiga

1. Idabelle is one of a group of popular witches at Pearl Peak Academy called The Points. They are called The Points because they wear pointy witch hats to prove they've travelled up the pipes to scare human children, which isn't allowed.

2. Her favourite shop in Pearl Peak is Squeal Records, which sells lots of old music and chunky earrings.

3. She secretly likes working at the First Witch Who Landed in Sinkville Historical site because she likes how quiet it is, and she can practise spells and not have to be popular.

4. Her best friend is Melodie McDamp, who is also in The Points.

5. She and Melodie are saving up their money from their weekend jobs to make their own line of earrings called Bling by Bat & McDamp.

How to Make Splat Cakes

WHAT YOU'LL NEED:

For the batter

- ☆ 110 g butter
- ☆ 110 g caster sugar
- ☆ 2 free-range eggs
- ☆ 1 tsp vanilla extract
- ☆ 110 g self-raising flour

For the icing

- ☆ 140 g butter
- ☆ 280 g icing sugar
- ☆ 1 tbsp milk
- ☆ Black food colouring

☆ Chocolate sprinkles

☆ Chocolate balls

☆ Chocolate buttons

☆ Edible glitter

HOW TO MAKE THEM:

Cake bit

1. Preheat the oven to 180°C/350°F/gas 4.

2. Cream the butter and sugar together in a bowl. Beat in the eggs and stir in the vanilla extract.

3. Fold in the flour.

4. Spoon the mixture into paper cases.

5. Bake in the oven for 10–15 minutes, or until golden-brown on top.

6. Set aside to cool.

Icing bit

1. Beat the butter in a large bowl until soft.

2. Add half the icing sugar and beat until smooth.

3. Add the rest of the icing sugar with the milk (add more if necessary).

4. Add a couple of drops of black food colouring.

Cake assembly bit

1. Now scrunch up your fist and – SPLAT. Squash the cakes.

2. Spoon some icing on to each of them.

3. Add chocolate sprinkles and round chocolate balls and buttons (so it looks a little like rocky ground), and finish with edible glitter.

Cat Hospital in the Towers

Unfortunately, the shortcut led to Sinkville's only cat hospital.

Lizzie Beast, however, was *fine*, once they gave her seven stiches and removed the cat ears that had accidentally been transplanted on to her head.

Tiga winced as she made her way down the corridor. The meows in the cat hospital were shrill, and for some reason every witch was bewitched to look like a gigantic mouse walking on two legs and wearing a doctor's coat, which just made the whole place seem like one big nightmare.

'Right, Lizzie Beast is not, as we suspected, dead or maimed, so it's time I returned home,' Felicity Bat said, making for the window.

'I can't believe Idabelle shoved us down that hole,' Fran cried.

'Thanks for being nice to us, Felicity,' Tiga said with a smile.

'Oh please,' Felicity Bat said, jumping out of the window and hovering effortlessly. 'I'm never nice. See you at Witchoween.'

'We need to find that micro cat,' Fran hissed in Tiga's ear. 'It knows too much. It must be in here somewhere.'

A witch bewitched to look like a mouse toddled past pushing a cart crammed full of cats.

'It's not going to be easy to find,' Tiga said. 'Where's Fluffanora?'

'In her trunk,' Fran said, pointing to where it sat below the window.

A letter came gliding past and slotted neatly into the side of the trunk's hatch. Tiga watched as it was yanked inside. It was purple, with the unmistakeable messy handwriting of Peggy.

'What's wrong with your face?' Fran said, zooming up close to Tiga.

Tiga lowered her voice to a fairy-level whisper. 'I think Fluffanora and Peggy are up to something. I have a feeling … Fluffanora was being weird at the *Toad* magazine offices. She was very defensive about what Peggy was doing, as if Peggy was doing *something* and she didn't want me to know about it.'

'Hmm,' Fran said, furrowing her brow like she did when she starred in the fairy detective drama *Detective Buzz: Is it a bee? Is it a wasp? No, it's a fairy who can only say buzz (because she had an accident when she was a teenager and forgot every single word, except for buzz).*

Lizzie Beast came limping down the hall and picked up the camera. 'So sorry about that.'

'Just don't do it again,' Fran said.

'Fran!' Tiga cried. 'Lizzie Beast nearly died. And that wasn't her fault.'

'I have an idea,' Fran said excitedly. 'Ready the camera, Lizzie Beast.'

Tiga sighed as Fran started making irritating warm-up gurgling noises.

'HERE WE ARE, IN THE CAT HOSPITAL!' Fran

cheered. 'But we aren't here to tell you all about it. We're here to hunt down the micro cat. So come with us on this exciting adventure!

Nomicrocats were har med during the making of this do cumentary.'

'Sorry, CUT!' Tiga said, her eyes wide. 'What did you say at the end?'

'No-micro-cats-were-harmed-during-the-making-of-this-documentary,' Fran repeated more slowly. 'For legal reasons.'

A tiny grey cat next to them meowed cutely.

'This is Dust,' a squat little witch doctor explained, her mouse nose twitching. 'She's been at the hospital for two weeks now. She's a stray, so we're hoping someone can adopt her.'

Fran looked lovingly at the cat. Tiga had never seen Fran look lovingly at anything like that – except her own face in the mirror, or her reflection in a mirror, or her reflection in Julie Jumbo Wings' caravan, or Crispy's caravan, or her reflection in Tiga's eyeball. Any reflection of herself, really.

'I wish I could take Dust home with me,' Fran said, 'but she'll grow bigger and eventually eat me. But I can help! We shall add an appeal to my fans! FAAAAAAANS! Dust has been here for two weeks and needs a loving home,' Fran said, looking into the camera, her eyes big and filled with tears.

Tiga could feel her eyes welling up. Fran was good.

'And Dust also needs a makeover,' Fran said, taking it in an inappropriate direction.

'I don't think Dust really does need a makeov–' the witch doctor tried.

'SILENCE, NOVICE!' Fran roared, flicking her finger and covering Dust in glittery dust. 'Dust shall henceforth be called not Dust but GLITTERYDUST! If you think you can give Glitterydust a home –'

Glitterydust looked annoyed to be covered in glitter.

'– then fly on down to the cat hospital!'

☆⟡☆

The next room was the worst.

'This, viewers,' Fran whispered, her face practically

160

touching the camera, 'is the Plaster Room.'

Tiga ducked as a large plaster went soaring magically through the air and tried to fix itself to a cat. The room was barely a room at all – more a mass of flying plasters covered in cat hair, and a lot of angry cats. Tiga was sidestepping slowly towards a tiny pot of wobbling jam. Fran had given her a mission: catch the micro cat. The whole Plaster Room scene was a setup. They knew the micro cat was in there, now they just had to catch it.

'The Plaster Room was built ten years ago by a witch called Sticky Berta. Most witches believe plasters are no good for cats, except for pulling off their hair, but Sticky Berta believed otherwise and so here we are – NOW, TIGA!' Fran roared.

Tiga dived for the jam jar and caught hold of it, along with something small and wriggly.

'I have the micro cat!' she announced triumphantly, before the little thing leapt at her, sending her tumbling forward.

Fran flew over to Lizzie Beast and flicked on the camera.

Tiga rolled around, wrestling with it, hair flying everywhere.

'This is award-winning footage,' Fran whispered to Lizzie Beast. 'You couldn't fake this action.'

Tiga went crashing through a large window and into the next room, where a bunch of witches bewitched to look like mice were tucking cats into little beds.

The cats looked horrified.

Tiga rolled from left to right, knocking beds over and sending cats tumbling, while the mice doctors scuttled around squeak-screaming.

'What dress are you going to wear to the award ceremony?' Fran asked Lizzie Beast. 'I think I'll wear my sparkly blue one because it'll go with the Best Action Film trophy, which also happens to be blue and sparkly.'

There was a loud clanging noise as a cat pelted into the kitchen next door.

'Erm,' Fran said, scanning the room. 'We seem to have lost Tiga.'

Slowly, like a hero, Tiga emerged, fur-covered and scratched, from the pile of cats in the centre of the room.

She held up a fist in triumph. 'I have the micro cat,' she wheezed. 'I HAVE THE MICRO CAT!'

'Bravo!' Fran said, zooming about her head and clapping loudly. So loudly it momentarily startled Tiga, and with one swift movement the micro cat leapt from her grasp and dived straight up –

☆⭐☆

It turns out there is one thing that will make Fluffanora roar with laughter. And that thing is an X-ray of Tiga with a micro cat lodged up her nose.

*[THERE IS NO FOOTAGE OF THIS INCIDENT,
BECAUSE IT WAS NOT PRETTY]*

Five Things You Didn't Know About Sticky Berta, by Tiga (for fun)

1. Sticky Berta has one blue eye and one brown eye.

2. She invented cat plasters – they peel off without balding the cat.

3. She knows where Lumpy the cat is but refuses to reveal the location to Aggie Hoof.

4. She believes that cats make witches happier. Unless the cat is mean.

5. She wrote the jingle to the Sticky Berta Cat Plaster advert, featuring a soft flute and cats wailing.

16

The Cauldron Islands

'I need a holiday after that,' Tiga said, rubbing her red nose. 'I think there's a micro claw still stuck up there.'

'Well then,' Fran said with a smile. 'The next place on the list is perfect for a holiday! A great place to unwind and recover from a micro cat to the nose.'

'THE CAUDRON ISLANDS!' Tiga cheered.

Lizzie Beast nodded and pulled out a bottle of Flappy Flora's Sloppy Suncream. Tiga stared at it, intrigued. She thought they'd stopped making Flappy Flora's floral products, because it was a really difficult brand name to say.

'I *HATE* THE CAULDRON ISLANDS,' Fluffanora screamed.

Tiga patted her on the shoulder. 'Yes, we all know about your irrational hatred of the Cauldron Islands.'

'But,' Fluffanora added quietly, 'I do really want to know who the "confidential for security reasons" witch is.'

'Me too!' Tiga said, as the four of them skipped out of the door to the sound of a thousand shrill miaows.

☆⍻☆

Tiga pulled some cool pastel-pink sunglasses and a pineapple-patterned headband from Fluffanora's trunk and strolled out to where the others were standing by the shore of Bubble Beach.

'We need to find Upper Cave Four,' Tiga said, tapping the list in her notebook.

Fran rolled over on her floating sun lounger. 'Do we?'

'Let's do it,' Fluffanora said, finishing off her Clutterbucks and dusting the sand off her skirt.

Lizzie Beast was nearly one hundred per cent Flappy Flora's Sloppy Suncream. Just two eyeballs and sun-cream. She was barely recognisable as a witch at all. She did the thumbs up.

A drumming sound started up nearby.

'Who is making that racket?' Fran scoffed, lifting her sunglasses on to her head and squinting through the sunlight.

Tiga, Fluffanora and Lizzie Beast shrugged.

'Ah,' Fluffanora said, clicking her fingers. 'That's the Silver Rats.'

The Silver Rats had recently become the biggest and bestselling band in Sinkville. Fluffanora wasn't a fan.

'I love them!' Tiga cried. She had been a huge fan of the Silver Rats ever since Aggie Hoof made Felicity Bat listen to all their albums, who then made Peggy listen to them, who then made Tiga listen to them.

She made her way over to a cluster of caves. 'It sounds live,' she said excitedly as she climbed up on the rocks, being careful not to fall. They were covered in lazing frogs. 'Pardon me, sorry, excuse me,' she mumbled.

Someone started singing in the cave.

'IT'S THEM!' Lizzie Beast roared, mowing Tiga down as she raced for the cave. Tiga got to her feet and scuttled after her – the rocks slippery and slimy underfoot.

'TIGA!' Fluffanora shouted, racing after her. 'WAIT FOR ME!'

Fran came gliding after them in her swimming costume.

Tiga rounded the corner and saw multicoloured lights streaming from one of the caves.

'QUICKLY!' Lizzie Beast yelled back to them. 'You don't want to miss filming this!'

☆⭐☆

The Silver Rats were recording their new album, *Broomstick in Your Soup*. The first song on the album was also called 'Broomstick in Your Soup' and went something like:

Soup! Soup! You've got broomstick in your soup!

'Hate it,' Fran muttered under her breath to Fluffanora, who nodded in agreement.

'Ah,' Tiga said. 'It's confidential because you're so famous.'

168

Big Ratty, the lead singer, nodded. 'Yeah, and we don't want people knowing we record in this cave – you'll need to keep it a secret.'

Lizzie Beast set up the camera with a dazed look on her face.

'You're putting it together all wrong!' Fran fussed around her, moving bits into place while Lizzie Beast stared ahead, as if in a trance. 'Really, Lizzie,' Fran said. 'I don't see why you're star-struck around these amateurs when you spend all your time with famous *me*!'

'We're here,' Tiga said into the camera, 'with the Silver Rats!'

Fran had let her present because she wasn't all that fussed about the Silver Rats.

'Their names are Big Ratty, Tails and Jam Jar, but their real names are Lydia Claw, Gemma Grey and Annie Legs, although no one is allowed to call them by their real names. Big Ratty is the lead singer, and she only wears clothes that have fallen from the pipes and been redesigned by a witch called Scissors who lives in a small invisible house in the forest.'

Big Ratty stared at her, the silver paint that covered her face glistening. 'Where did you hear that rubbish?'

Tiga cursed Aggie Hoof under her breath. 'Just … somewhere … not important.'

The three of them began to tune their instruments, singing loudly as they did so.

'I just have a couple of standard Witchoween questions,' Tiga said, the piece of paper in her hand shaking as she held it up. 'Any of you can answer. Question number one, what top tip would you give a witch who would like to have a job like yours?'

'Write all your thoughts down,' Jam Jar said. 'Fill notebooks with lyric ideas.'

'What object,' Tiga asked, 'would you never part with?'

'My Silver Rats hat, of course,' Big Ratty said. 'We had them specially made by Mrs Brew in Ritzy City. She got the rats ears just right.'

'And finally,' Tiga said, clearing her throat. 'What toothpaste do you use?'

'Slimeeze,' Big Ratty said. 'Because they have

limited-edition tubes that sing our songs while you brush your teeth.'

'Well, we've seen enough here!' Fran shouted, fingers in her ears.

'No!' Tiga cried.

Fran shrugged, her fingers still in her ears. 'I DIDN'T CATCH A WORD OF THAT!'

Fluffanora scooped the little fairy from the air and stuffed her in the trunk. It started shaking violently.

'Ah,' Fluffanora said, sitting on it. 'That's better.'

The Silver Rats all turned at once to face them, in that cool, coordinated, only-the-Silver-Rats-can-turn-like-that way. Tiga really wanted the rat ears they had on their hats.

'Maybe they can help,' Big Ratty said.

Jam Jar smiled.

'We have a problem,' Tails said. 'We're stuck. We've run out of juice.'

'I'll go get some Clutterbucks,' Fluffanora said efficiently, getting up from the trunk.

'No, not drinking juice,' Jam Jar said coolly. 'Song

juice. Creative juice. We can't think of the final song for the album.'

'Well,' Tiga said. 'I'm sure … we could help?'

'Are you musician witches too?' Big Ratty asked. 'Are you that new band, Flat Hat Bat Parade?

Tiga shook her head.

'Sometimes when I run my hair through my teeth it makes a musical sound,' Lizzie Beast said.

Fluffanora groaned.

'No …' Big Ratty said, flicking her finger and making a series of jam jars appear. 'I like that!'

'Like what?' Tiga said, as Big Ratty began to tap the jam jars, making a tune.

> *Hair and teeth make musical sounds*
> *Musical sounds*
> *Hair and teeth*
> *Lizzie Beast*
> *Musical sounds*

'I can't believe you like this band,' Fluffanora whispered

to Tiga. 'What is *wrong* with you?'

> *Little fairy in a trunk,*
> *Swimming costume*
> *Fairy trunk*
> *Armbands on*
> *Nowhere to go*
> *Small mouth*
> *Shrill fairy sounds*

'It's experimental music,' Tiga said defensively.

> *Fairy sounds*
> *From the trunk*
> *Eeeeeear paaaaain.*

'Well, I think we got it,' Big Ratty said, pulling off her hat and smudging her silver make-up. 'We'll call it "Lizzie Long Hair and the Swimming Fairy".'

'You've got a Silver Rats song named after you!' Tiga said, her shoulders sagging slightly with the weight of

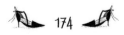

gigantic jealousy. 'A SILVER RATS SONG NAMED AFTER YOU!'

Lizzie Beast grinned and turned purple, clearly pleased with herself, but also hugely embarrassed by all the attention.

Fran crossed her arms angrily inside the trunk, making her armbands squeak. '*Swimming fairy?* It's Fran the *FABULOUS* fairy, thank you.'

Five Things You Didn't Know About The Silver Rats, by Tiga

1. They do secret concerts around Sinkville. They bewitch a puddle and you jump through it to get to the concert. Only superfans know how to identify a Silver Rats puddle from a regular puddle.

2. Their superfans are called Wigglers.

3. Their bestselling song, 'I Want to Curse Your Loved Ones', accidentally made its way above the pipes, and

was played on human radio, cursing millions. The spell was, thankfully, quickly reversed by Gretal Green at NAPA.

4. They travel in a bewitched pumpkin shaped like a rat. It can fly two thousand times faster than a broom.

5. Big Ratty's aunt is Bettie Cranberry in the Coves. It's rumoured that's where the Silver Rats live – although they refuse to confirm or deny these claims.

How to Write a Song for Your Party

The host of the Witchoween party should fill in the blanks, along with three other guests, and everyone sings:

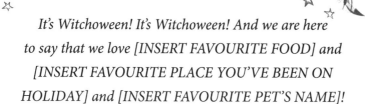

It's Witchoween! It's Witchoween! And we are here to say that we love [INSERT FAVOURITE FOOD] and [INSERT FAVOURITE PLACE YOU'VE BEEN ON HOLIDAY] and [INSERT FAVOURITE PET'S NAME]!

(Sing the host's version first, then guest one, then guest two, then guest three, then finish with the host's version again – but this time shout it.)

The Coves!

Fluffanora was trying to balance on the bucking trunk.

'Let her out,' Tiga said warily. 'And stand back.'

Fluffanora flipped the trunk open and Fran came whizzing out, screaming at Fluffanora,

'YOULOCKEDMEINTHEREANDYOUCAN'T DOTHATYOUSHOULDGOTOPRISON –'

'The Silver Rats made up a song and it's sort of about you,' Fluffanora said casually.

Fran fell to the floor with a bang, clutching her heart. She reached up a tiny little hand. 'FAME,' she gasped as she grabbed at the air.

'She says *thank you*,' Tiga said to the Silver Rats.

Jam Jar forced a smile. 'Where are you off to for

your documentary next?' she asked Tiga.

'Oh,' Tiga said with a goofy smile as she checked her notebook. 'The Coves. It was my favourite part of the Witch Wars competition.'

'Ah,' Big Ratty said. 'You're Tiga from Witch Wars. I knew I recognised your face. We all wanted you to win. Well, Tiga, you're in luck, because this little cave has a secret passage and I think you'll like where it leads …'

'Well, I was not aware of this secret passage!' Fran said as they all made their way down the dark and winding secret passageway the Silver Rats had shown them. 'And I know almost all the secret places in Sinkville. Even I'm learning things from this documentary, and *I'm* making it.'

'SOMETHING JUST TOUCHED MY FACE,' Fluffanora shouted.

'It's probably just the cool air,' Tiga said, although she was sure something had touched her face too. It was definitely getting colder – they were making their way from the Cauldron Islands back to the mainland.

'If this is leading us where I think it's leading us, then it's going to take us about ten hours to walk,' Fluffanora said.

'I'll magic the trunk!' Fran cried from the darkness ahead. 'Then you can all sit on it and zip along – we'll be there in no time!'

FIVE SECONDS LATER ...

'I am many excellent things,' Fran said boastfully as they emerged from the tunnel. 'And efficient is one of them.'

Fluffanora plonked the trunk down and stared up at the large, dark house that towered above them.

They had arrived at the exact spot Tiga had hoped to see.

'ECHO!' Tiga cried.

Echo echo echo echo went the cave.

'NO ONE CALLED ECHO LIVES HERE, GO AWAY!' came a cry as the door to the rambling old house was flung open.

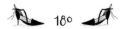

'Lily Cranberry!' Tiga cried, racing over to the witch and giving her a big hug.

'I'm ready for my Witchoween close-up,' Lily said.

'No matter how much I learn about this place, and the fact that it's not a dangerous cove but is actually filled with wonderful witches, it still never fails to creep me out,' Fluffanora whispered to Tiga as Lily's sister Bettie trotted out of the house, grabbed the trunk and chucked it effortlessly through the window in the highest turret!

'It's the cake and fun,' she said as they all stared at her in amazement. She leaned forward and flexed her bicep in Tiga's face. 'Gives you muscles.'

☆⭐☆

'ACTION!' Fran roared. She'd decided to direct this one.

'First question,' Tiga said. 'What's your favourite party game?'

'I'll show you!' Lily Cranberry said, making off down the corridor. She stopped about halfway and stomped five times on the carpet.

'What *are* you doing?' Fran said, sounding spooked.

There was a creaking sound and the carpet rolled away obediently, revealing a trapdoor.

Tiga knelt down and slowly lifted it. Beneath it lay a sparkly slide.

'Well go on!' Lily Cranberry cried, pushing the little witch head first down it.

Tiga grinned as she went flying, her skirt around her neck, her heart beating in what felt like her nose. Down and down she went in a perfectly straight line, landing with a crunch in a room filled with partying witches. She got to her feet and cheered!

The witches in the room all threw their arms in the air and cheered back.

Fluffanora and Fran came tumbling after her, followed by Lizzie Beast, who was rolling in a perfect circle, so when she crashed into the crowd of cheering witches she knocked all but two of them over, like an excellent bowling ball.

In the middle of the room was a table, and on it, a pair of gloves, a witch's hat, a cape, a spoon and a gigantic seven-tiered black cake covered in sprinkles.

'It's a new game!' Lily Cranberry cried. 'Possibly our best party game yet. We call it Cake Witch Five.'

'Why five?' Fluffanora asked.

Bettie Cranberry produced a glossy black die from her pocket. 'Because five is the magic number. At least in this game anyway. All you have to do is take it in turns to roll the die. If you roll a five, you have to dart over to the table, put on the outfit and eat as much cake as you can with the spoon before one of the other competitors rolls a five.'

Fran rubbed her hands together with glee. 'Lizzie Beast, START ROLLING!'

Lizzie Beast curled up in a ball. The witches groaned and quickly took a step backwards.

'No,' Fran said faintly. 'Roll the camera. Get the camera rolling. You know, *film it.*'

'Oh,' Lizzie Beast said, sheepishly getting to her feet. 'Of course.'

The game was a fix. Fran rolled a five every time. And

every time she did so, there was a suspicious puff of glittery dust.

'Fran, you're cheating!' Tiga cried.

'*Mhumf?*' Fran said, her cheeks packed full of cake.

'You look like an above-the-pipes hamster,' Fluffa-nora said.

Fran shrugged and kept on eating.

'It's important to remember,' Lily said into the camera, 'that the first rule of cake is to put in lots of things that you like, then it will always taste good. For example, jam, chocolate, dancing.'

'How can you put dancing in a cake?' Tiga asked.

The other witches cackled.

'No, seriously,' Tiga said.

'Oh. Well, you just …' She put an elbow in the centre of the cake, knocking Fran out of the way, and jiggled it. 'Now it has dancing in it.'

Five Things You Didn't Know About Lily Cranberry, by Tiga

1. Lily Cranberry thought of the band name the Silver Rats.

2. She holds the record for hosting the longest party (894 years).

3. She considers every day Witchoween in the Coves and believes every witch should be celebrated and feel special every day.

4. She has fallen head first into cakes 894 times.

5. She uses the secret passage to holiday on the Cauldron Islands, where she pretends her name is Pamela-Patricia Crumpet-Darling.

How to Play the Cove Witches' Cake-Eating Party Game

WHAT YOU'LL NEED:
- ☆ A pair of gloves
- ☆ A witch's hat
- ☆ A cape
- ☆ A spoon

☆ A gigantic seven-tiered multicoloured, black-sprinkle-covered cake (or something smaller if you don't have time)

☆ A die

HOW TO PLAY:

☆ Each contestant rolls the die. If you roll a five, you dart over to the cake, put on the witch items and begin eating the cake with a spoon.

☆ Meanwhile, all the other competitors continue rolling the die. When someone else rolls a five, the person in the witch costume eating the cake has to STOP and switch places with the witch who rolled the five. The new witch who rolled the five now races to put on all the witch items and eat the cake with the spoon.

☆ The aim of the game is to get the most cake.

☆ Make sure to roll the die as fast as you can!

18

Gretal Green in NAPA

Getting to the next stop – Silver City – was easy from the coves. Lily Cranberry bewitched one of the four-poster beds in the house and they flew straight there on it.

Tiga could tell her mum was surprised when a gigantic bed filled with witches landed outside her office, but she managed to keep a straight face.

'I feel very lucky to be in the Witchoween documentary this year,' Gretal Green said modestly. 'What a treat!'

'We'll need to film some of your inventions,' Fran said, bossily pushing her way inside. 'And you'll need to explain what they are because they are all odd and I can't make head nor cat's tail of them!'

Gretal Green smiled and led them towards her office.

Tiga was always very proud of how impressed her friends were when they saw it.

'Wow,' Lizzie Beast said as she stepped inside.

'Oh no! Don't say WOW,' Gretal Green said, ducking as a giant pipe glided across the roof and ground to a halt above Lizzie Beast.

Lizzie Beast looked up slowly.

'I … just … Um,' Gretal Green said, trying to push the pipe with a flick of her finger.

There was a hiss. A gurgle.

A tonne of water came shooting out, and then SPLOOOOSH.

Lizzie Beast stood motionless and stiff, her long hair sodden and draped over her face. A small puddle sat at her feet.

'The Witch-o-Wash,' Gretal Green said sheepishly. 'You say w-o-w to summon it.'

Fran clapped enthusiastically. 'Bravo! Now you need to make a small one for fairies. I'd drown in that one – oh, *WOW*, was that a lot of water!'

'NO!' the witches cried.

☆⇆☆⋆

Fran hovered in the corner, sulkily wringing out her skirt. She hadn't drowned, which was the main thing. Her beehive was soaked and lopsided, so she insisted Tiga do the presenting for this one. Plus, it was Tiga's mum. And Fran was now scared of the gadgets.

Gretal Green showed Tiga a very slick black jump-suit. 'This is our latest spy suit for above the pipes. It comes with human-style trainers that can make the wearer invisible at the flick of a finger, and we've rejigged the slugs so they can travel on a little leash with the spy witch and morph into any pet that fits the setting – a sausage dog for London, a cow for the country.'

'I don't … think humans, um, *walk* cows on leashes.'

'Or even a crocodile for more exotic locations.'

'Again,' Tiga said, 'um, I don't think humans *walk* crocodiles. In fact, I *know* they don't walk croc–'

'And what's this?' Fran said grumpily, pointing at a tray of sweets and chocolate.

'Oh,' Gretal Green said. 'That's an exact replica of what

was stolen from the sweet shop above the pipes … by Mrs Clutterbuck. You see, she tried to pay in sinkels and they wouldn't accept them, so she ran. It's created a problem because now the humans are investigating a robbery and trying to figure out where sinkels came from. I've been recruited by Peggy and the Witch Order to fix the situation. I can't talk about it on camera.'

'Is the Witch Order like the magic police?' Fluffanora asked, completely gripped.

Gretal Green nodded. 'Mrs Clutterbuck's trip above the pipes has been branded a CODE Y, which is serious. Not her fault though! And I hear the cocktails she's made from her stolen goods are truly delicious! Oh, do you want to see my cool pen?'

'What does it do?' Fluffanora asked excitedly.

'WARDROBE!' Fran snapped. 'Less yapping. You work behind the scenes.'

Fluffanora stuck out her tongue.

'THE GREATEST INSULT!' Fran roared. 'Did anyone see that?'

'So,' Tiga said, trying to move things along. 'The pen.'

'It's a travel pen. I call it Travelpenpen.'

Tiga looked bored. 'It's a pen you can carry when you're travelling? That's not that great.'

'No,' Gretal Green said casually. 'You draw wherever you want to travel to, and then it takes you there.'

'NO WAY!' Fluffanora cried, zipping in front of the camera and grabbing the pen.

'I give up,' Fran said, pinching the bridge of her nose. 'I just … amateurs.'

'Why don't you try it?' Gretal Green said. 'Where's your next stop?'

'We're going to Brew's to interview Fluffanora's mum,' Tiga said, brandishing her notebook.

Fluffanora bit her lip and began carefully sketch-ing the outside of Brew's in the air in front of them. The pen ink was dark and gloopy. When she finished, the drawing began to flash.

'Step on through,' Gretal Green said with a wink.
And just like that, they were gone.

Five Things You Didn't Know About Gretal Green, by Tiga

1. Gretal Green's work at NAPA (the National Above the Pipes Association) has transformed witch science, linking it with human science in magical ways. This year she will receive the Top Witch Award of Wonderfulness at a special ceremony.

2. She believes in telling certain human children about witches and the world below the pipes, in the hope that one day humans and witches can exist together peacefully.

3. She has burnt her eyebrows 2,599 times.

4. She has a team of two thousand witches who help develop NAPA projects. She hopes to double that

number this year and find more young witches who would like to get jobs in science.

5. Her best friend is Mrs Brew. They have matching best-friend gloves that have been specially customised with a spell to wriggle off the wearer's hand and collect cakes, pies and tarts when commanded.

How to Make a Witchoween Drawing Wall and Party Pen

Every good Witchoween party features a large piece of paper on the wall. Guests are encouraged to draw fun things (or just write notes and their names). Witches often write why they think their fellow witches are fabulous, while some draw pineapples. So stick a piece of paper to the wall, and then spruce up your pen to make it extra Witchoweeny. Unfortunately, it probably won't be a transporting pen like Gretal Green's, because she's a scientist and makes these things in a controlled lab with strict health and safety restrictions in place.

WHAT YOU'LL NEED:

- ☆ A pen
- ☆ Two fabric strips – one about an inch thick, the other twice as thick
- ☆ Glue (glue guns are best)
- ☆ Scissors
- ☆ Needle and thread

HOW TO MAKE IT

1. Add a bit of glue at one end of the pen, and fix the thinner fabric strip to it. Wrap it around, gluing as you go. The pen should now be covered in the fabric.

2. Fold over the second piece of fabric and cut a fringe into the open side.

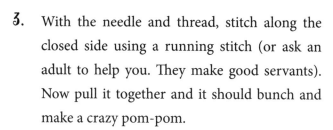

3. With the needle and thread, stitch along the closed side using a running stitch (or ask an adult to help you. They make good servants). Now pull it together and it should bunch and make a crazy pom-pom.

4. Glue the crazy pom-pom to the top of the pen.

19

Mrs Brew at the Brews' Studio

They didn't quite arrive at Brew's, but emerged from the drawing at the Wartwell & Witch Toy Store, which was about five minutes down the road in a very similar-looking building.

'Oh look,' Tiga said. 'Wartell & Witch, I've never noticed that toy shop before – that must be where Felicity Bat gets all those cuddly spiders.'

The four of them charged up the road, past the witches dining outside the cafés and reading the latest *Ritzy City Post*.

They stopped outside Brew's. 'Why is the lamp post wearing a dress?' Tiga asked.

Fluffanora shook her head and walked in. 'You don't want to know!'

☆⳽☆

Mrs Brew's studio was one of Tiga's favourite places in Ritzy City. Around the edges were rails of half-made dresses and piles of hats, and the back wall – known as the Embellishment Wall – was stacked high with containers full of beads and gemstones and pearls and feathers and buttons. And in the middle sat Mrs Brew's huge desk, illuminated by the huge, round window that looked down on the busy Ritzy City streets outside.

'I thought we'd make some couture hats,' Mrs Brew said. She flicked her finger and four black hats landed in front of them with a bang, plus a tiny one for Fran.

'You could just set your camera up there,' Mrs Brew suggested to Lizzie Beast, 'then you can join in too.'

Fran was about to protest that the camera would have to move and zoom and such, but Tiga distracted her with a tube of glitter.

'So, Mrs Brew,' Fran said as they got stuck into designing their hats. 'What advice would you give to any young witches who want to be fashion designers?'

Mrs Brew glued some gemstones around the rim of her hat. 'Well, I'd say, practise on yourself first. I was always altering my own outfits as a young witch – adding furry cuffs to a cardigan, gluing little gemstones to the pockets on my jackets, dyeing the laces on my boots. Start designing your clothes now, and keep a notebook with all the things you've done!'

Tiga and Fluffanora came back from the Embellishment Wall with armfuls of stuff.

'I'm going to make little glittery slugs and sew them all over my hat,' Tiga said.

'I'm going to completely cover mine in pom-poms,' Fluffanora said as Fran dropped the feather she was about to glue on to her hat and picked up some pom-poms instead.

'And who is your favourite designer at the moment?' Fran asked.

'Now that's a good question,' Mrs Brew said. 'I would say Paisley Parade; she makes couture shoes in Silver City. She adds lots of colourful embellishment and fun laces. Some have magic elements, like self-tying laces, and patterns that change colour. I think she made a pair that shouts directions if you get lost. She's just about to open her first shop; she's taking over Shoes by Karen. I predict this time next year every witch in Sinkville will be wearing a pair of Paisley Parade shoes.'

'FINISHED!' Fran roared, holding up her pom-pom hat. It was virtually identical to Fluffanora's.

'Wonderful!' Mrs Brew said, admiring their creations. Lizzie Beast had gone for neon ribbons, Tiga was sparkly slugs and polka dots, and Mrs Brew had made a striking silver-embroidered one, with gemstone edging.

'Where are you off to next?' she asked.

Tiga opened up her notebook. 'We're going to see Trilly at her tea shop in the forest.'

'Oh, well in that case, I'll drive you! I've been meaning to take Ratty Ann for a spin.'

'Who is Ratty Ann?' Lizzie Beast asked.

'It's her car,' Fran said with a scoff. 'Can't believe you don't know that. Mrs Brew is *famous*.'

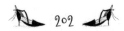

Five Things You Didn't Know About Mrs Brew, by Tiga

1. Mrs Brew was given Ratty Ann as a birthday present, from Freddie Crow, the witch who owns Crow's Toes in Pearl Peak.

2. Her favourite book is called *The Witch in Wardrobe*, about a small witch who lives in a world called Wardrobe.

3. In the morning, she drinks Jumpjam Juice, which is a blend of jam and raw frog tears.

4. Every year she attends the Glamour Gala, a dinner and ball featuring all the top designers and stars of Sinkville. They wear incredible outfits, and the designers compete to see who can come up with the most creative design.

5. She likes to dress up the lamp post outside her shop, just for fun. She calls her Lanky Lorna.

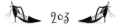

How to Decorate Your Shoes
Like Paisley Parade

WHAT YOU'LL NEED:

- ☆ A pair of plain shoes or trainers (preferably white fabric)
- ☆ Glue
- ☆ Laces (preferably white fabric)
- ☆ Felt pens in different colours
- ☆ Pom-poms
- ☆ Gems
- ☆ Some real or fake flowers
- ☆ Glitter (in assorted colours)
- ☆ Any other things you fancy sticking to your shoes

HOW TO MAKE THEM:

GO NUTS. Paisley Parade is excellent at creating unique designs – glitter-covered trainers with flowers glued to the tongue and multicoloured striped laces coloured in with pens. One of her popular designs features blue laces and black glitter stars with pompoms around the edge of the shoes.

You can design them however you want – and they will look FABULOUS.

Trilly's Tea in the Forest

They waved goodbye to Mrs Brew and made their way through Ritzy City and into the forest. Tiga helped Fluffanora carry her trunk, walking in silence, while Fran whistled the theme tune for *Cooking for Tiny People*.

Up ahead Tiga could see a replica of Peggy's shoe house. The same shoe house she and Peggy had slept in during Witch Wars.

> *Little laces and heels in a heap,*
> *Make me a better place to sleep!*

The sound of Peggy cheerily chirping the spell echoed in Tiga's head.

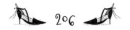

'They made a replica of the shoe as a tourist attraction,' Fran explained. 'Witches come from all over Sinkville to stay in it and pretend to be you and Peggy!'

'Well, that's not weird at all,' Tiga said.

'The shoe house is so popular it's booked up seven months in advance!' Fran went on. 'There's a huge waiting list. Lovely Trilly of Trilly's Tea fame looks after it.'

Lizzie Beast shuddered. They were near the spot where she had crashed into a chandelier, squashing her best friend, Patty Pigeon, and knocking her out of the Witch Wars competition.

'How is Patty Pigeon?' Fluffanora asked, clearly thinking the same thing as Lizzie Beast.

'SHE'S ALIVE,' Lizzie Beast grunted defensively.

'Well, I assumed *that*,' Fluffanora said.

Up ahead, there was a little clearing in the forest. A small house sat surrounded by hanging vines and sweet black flowers.

There was a loud BANG, and a perfectly crisp *Toad* magazine landed with a thud on the trunk.

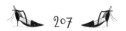

TOAD MAGAZINE

WHAT'S BEEN HOPPINING AROUND SINKVILLE!

ON A ROLL

According to our spy, the Witchoween documentary is on a roll! And Lizzie Beast, their camera witch, has been quite literally rolling – knocking over seventeen Cove witches in the process!

Fran began flying close to the ground, her fists grabbing at clumps of air. 'WHO LET THE MICRO CAT GO!' she roared.

'Fran,' Fluffanora said. '*You* were looking after the micro cat. You're pretty much the only one who can see it!'

Fran stopped and looked up. 'This feels like fairy discrimination. I'm not quite sure why. BUT IT DOES.'

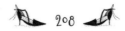

Fluffanora sighed. 'I'll be in my trunk. I can't deal with any more today.'

'BUT I NEED NEW BOOTS AND A HAIR WRAP!' Fran roared.

'What's all the racket out here then?' came a voice from the house.

'Hello, Trilly,' Fran said flatly. 'Sorry about Fluffanora.'

'Sorry about Flu–?!' Fluffanora began. But Tiga sat on the lid of the trunk before she could burst out of it.

'Do come in,' Trilly said kindly. 'I have something to show you!'

✫✫✫

'You bought the old Flappy Flora's Floral Foot Cream recipe and are going to remake it?' Tiga asked, picking up one of the jars. It had a picture of a foot on it, covered in flowers.

Trilly skipped around the room excitedly. 'Yes! I don't know why they stopped making it.'

'Because Flappy Flora's Floral Foot Cream is really hard to say,' Tiga, Lizzie and Fran said together. It

sounded like Fluffanora said it too, but it was difficult to tell from the muffled mumble that came from the trunk.

'Would you like a witch pedicure?' Trilly asked Tiga.

Tiga looked at Fran. 'Is it like an … above-the-pipes pedicure?'

Fran thought for a moment. 'Does an above-the-pipes pedicure involve sparkly black nail polish?'

'Could do,' Tiga said.

'And a cat?'

'No,' Tiga said.

'Well, then it's probably different,' Fran said.

Tiga looked nervously at Trilly, who was placing a little black basin next to a chair. 'Want one?' she asked Tiga.

'I …' Tiga began. 'Don't … think so?'

FIVE MINUTES LATER …

Tiga sat with her feet in a basin of Flappy Flora's Floral Foot Cream.

'Another cup of Trilly's Tea Punch?' Trilly asked, scooping some of the delicious stuff from a Crinkle Cauldron.

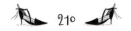

210

'Yes, please!' Tiga said as she flicked through her *Toad* magazine.

'Relaxing, isn't it?' Fran said. She was standing in the basin next to Tiga's feet, her legs completely covered in the cream.

Trilly poured a tiny amount of punch into an equally tiny cup and handed it to Fran.

Lizzie Beast zoomed the camera in on them.

'Trilly's Tea Retreat is a lovely way to spend a relaxing afternoon,' Fran said, taking a sip of the punch. 'I highly recommend her pedicures. And the Flappy Flora's Floral Foot Cream recipe has been altered, to smell less of feet and more of flowers, which –' She sniffed. 'Hasn't worked *at all*!'

Fluffanora peeked out of the trunk. 'I'm actually a bit jealous,' she whispered to Tiga. 'But if I come out then that means Fran wins.'

Tiga suddenly remembered something and looked up anxiously. 'Wait, when does the *cat* come into it?'

FIVE SECONDS AND A LOT OF FUR LATER …

211

'MAKE IT STOP!' Tiga roared as the cat rolled about on her feet, tickling her uncontrollably. 'THERE'S NO POINT TO THIS BIT!'

'It's a massage,' Trilly said, calmly lifting one of Tiga's feet and flicking her finger, covering her nails in a gorgeous, glittery black polish.

Tiga jolted in the seat, her eyes squeezed shut while the cat finished wriggling about on her other foot. 'MAKE THE CAT GO AWAY!'

Trilly flicked her finger and Tiga's other toes were perfectly painted too. Fran lay down in the thick cream bath and stuck her feet in the air. 'ME NEXT!'

The cat came galloping over.

'NOT THE CAT!' Fran quickly corrected herself. 'JUST THE POLISH! JUST THE POLISH!'

Five Things You Didn't Know About Trilly, by Tiga

1. Trilly has always lived in the forest and finds Ritzy City overwhelming.

2. She spreads her possessions across the forest, bewitching trees to act as cupboards. Every so often a witch will lean against one of the trees and a pile of pyjamas or dresses or board games will pop out.

3. Trilly's grandmother invented the very popular witch board game BROOMSTICK BOOM.

4. Her favourite plant is weeds.

5. Her pet plant is a weed called Creeper. She ties bows in his leaves to make him pretty.

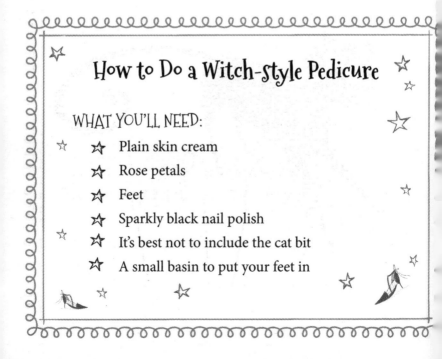

How to Do a Witch-style Pedicure

WHAT YOU'LL NEED:

- ☆ Plain skin cream
- ☆ Rose petals
- ☆ Feet
- ☆ Sparkly black nail polish
- ☆ It's best not to include the cat bit
- ☆ A small basin to put your feet in

HOW TO DO IT:

1. Put some cream in the basin.
2. Add the rose petals.
3. Put your feet in.
4. Swish them around, read a magazine, drink a glass of Trilly's punch.
5. Take your feet out and wipe them with a towel.
6. Paint your toenails with the sparkly polish.
7. Let it dry.

Cakes, Pies and That's About It Really

Tiga could see the rooftops of Ritzy City glinting up ahead, and no matter how many times she visited, the sight of the place made her tingle every time.

'I think we should go to Cakes, Pies and That's About It Really,' Fluffanora said, emerging from the trunk. 'We deserve it.'

'Yes!' Fran squealed. 'And we can film them making their special That's About It Really tarts, tell everyone the recipe and make me a hero.'

'It's not on my list ...' Tiga said.

'I just want something to eat,' Fluffanora grumbled.

'I'll need Wardrobe to get me a nice tart-themed hat,' Fran said.

Fluffanora marched on with purpose, pretending she couldn't hear her, and stormed through the door to Cakes, Pies and That's About It Really, making the witches inside jump.

'Afternoon,' Tiga said awkwardly. 'We're just going to … go back there … and –' She dived behind the counter and made her way through to the back.

They stopped and stared at all the witches racing around carrying pies. Huge conveyer belts were magic- ally suspended in the air, and all along them, That's About It Really tarts and fabulous cakes wobbled along and out to the front of the shop.

'Five pies for table ten!' came a shout.

'Black cake with jam glaze for table two!' came another.

Lizzie Beast hastily set up her camera and flicked it on.

'My hat! Hurry up, *Wardrobe*,' Fran hissed.

Fluffanora rolled her eyes and pulled a tiny hat from the trunk.

She smirked.

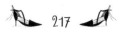

'What are you smirking at?' Tiga asked as Fran snatched the hat and put it on her head. 'Ah. I see what you've done.'

The hat was shaped like a tart and had NARF written on it. 'Narf' was Fran's least favourite word, because a long time ago, when Fran made her film debut in *Fly Like the Wind* (a classic about a fairy who unfortunately encounters a tornado), the director of the film spelled her name wrong on the credits at the end, writing it backwards. For four years, she was known as

Narf. It was a dark time for Fran.

'Here we are,' Fran said, completely unaware of her hat. 'In the famous Ritzy City bakery, Cakes, Pies and That's About It Really. Today we are behind the scenes, where we will teach you how to make the sensational and top secret That's About It Really tarts – only available in Ritzy City!'

'Ah ah ah, no filming in here!' said one of the bakers, putting a hand over the camera lens. She turned to Fran. 'Sorry … Narf, you can't film in here.'

'WHAT DID YOU CALL ME?!' Fran roared, her beehive bursting into flames.

TEN MINUTES AND ONE FIRE-
EXTINGUISHER SPELL LATER …

'And we didn't even get the secret recipe,' Fran said glumly, chucking the burnt Narf hat over her shoulder. 'Not getting the recipe is *even worse* than being called Narf for four years. That recipe would've made me a hero.'

'Where to now, Fran?' Fluffanora asked. Tiga could tell she felt bad about the Narf incident. Smoke coming out of Fran's ears was usually as angry as she got. They'd never seen her hair combust before.

Fran sighed and stared at the list. 'It's Mavis and her weird-shaped jam jars.'

Ritzytwig Theatre

Marge Mustoyd was the director of the Ritzytwig Theatre, Sinkville's oldest and grandest playhouse. Her latest production was days from launch, and Marge Mustoyd wasn't much in the mood for being interviewed.

'I'm sorry, you're going to have to forgive me, I'm very busy,' she fretted. She was tall and lean, with bright purple lipstick and square-cut glasses to match. She had stars on her smock and scribbles on her tights. 'I'm putting the finishing touches to *A Human Called Greg*.'

'What's it about?' Fran said, gesturing at Lizzie Beast to start rolling the camera.

'A human called Greg,' Marge Mustoyd said. 'He falls down the pipes into Sinkville and is told by a fairy that he must find his way to NAPA, as the witch there is the only one who can send him home – he has to follow the winding road.'

'That sounds familiar,' Tiga mumbled.

'Sorry, pardon me,' Fran said, zooming uncomfortably close to Marge Mustoyd's face. 'You mentioned a fairy at one point there. May I just enquire who is performing that role?'

'Ah, Julie,' Marge Mustoyd said, as Tiga, Lizzie Beast and Fluffanora took a cautious step back.

'Julie,' Fran said flatly. 'Julie.'

'Yes,' Marge Mustoyd said. 'Julie.'

'Julie Jumbo Wings?!' Fran cried.

'Well,' Marge Mustoyd said. 'I don't think that's what she goes by, though she does have rather large wi–'

'WELL JULIE JUMBO WINGS KEPT THIS QUIET!' Fran roared. 'How many lines does she have?'

'Fran …' Tiga said.

'And, more importantly,' Fran said, 'is it too late for me to audition?'

Marge Mustoyd rolled her eyes and stormed off.

'OR I COULD PLAY THE ROLE OF GREG?' Fran called after her. 'MOST WITCHES DON'T KNOW WHAT A HUMAN LOOKS LIKE ANYWAY! WE COULD TELL THEM HUMANS ARE VERY SMALL!'

☆⭐☆

'Well, you ruined that,' Tiga said. 'She's never going to come out of her office and speak to us.' She took a handful of black Ritzytwig popcorn and popped it in her mouth.

'All we have is footage of you begging to play the role

of a human called Greg,' Fluffanora added, taking a handful of popcorn too.

They sat in silence in the vast theatre. The seats were covered in the most beautiful black velvet, and the black velvet curtains that hung across the stage glinted with the glittery words *A Human Called Greg: A Ritzytwig Original.*

'I'll just have to really research the five things you didn't know about Marge Mustoyd and hope Patricia the producer is happy with it.'

Five Things You Didn't Know About Marge Mustoyd, by Tiga

1. Marge Mustoyd has written over fifty plays, and her most popular one is *Nightlight Cackle Feast*, which is played every Witchmas.

2. She wears a perfume called Mustoyd Deluxe, which was specially created for her by Whiffney's, the perfumery on Ritzy Lane.

3. She invented the recipe for the black popcorn at the Ritzytwig Theatre.

4. She draws patterns on her tights every morning depending on her mood. On good days it's little suns and rainbows, while on bad days it's usually really angry faces and lightning bolts.

5. Marge Mustoyd … rhymes with Large Crustoyd, which is a rare witch toe disease.

How to Create Marge Mustoyd-Style Tights Designs

WHAT YOU'LL NEED:

- ☆ A pair of black or white tights
- ☆ Some fabric pens

HOW TO MAKE THEM:

Design your tights! Marge Mustoyd likes to draw her mood – so you can draw smiley faces and sunshine and rainbows, or if you're furious right now, why not draw some thunderbolts and write *GRRR* on them? Or you can dream up your own design! Whatever you want.

Behind the Scenes at Mavis's Jam Stall

Mavis was pottering behind her jam stall, stacking jam jars in ambitious formations.

'You're here!' she cried when she saw the group of them coming down the road, like weathered travellers back from a lengthy adventure.

'I can't wait to show you this exciting new thing I've been working on,' Mavis said with a worrying grin.

'It's not weird-shaped jam jars again, is it?' Fluffanora said flatly.

Mavis blinked. 'No.'

'What is it, then?' Fran asked.

Mavis swallowed loudly. 'It's … nothing.'

Tiga started to laugh, but it was cut short when she tripped over something and went flying into Mavis's

stall. She grabbed a wobbling stack of jam jars to steady herself. 'What was that?' she said, turning to see that there was nothing on the ground for her to trip over at all. She reached down to see if she could feel anything, but Fluffanora grabbed her hand.

'NO! It was nothing. You tripped over nothing.'

'But –' Tiga began. 'It felt hard … and lumpy.'

'It was just your chunky boot,' Fluffanora said, with what Tiga was sure was a hint of panic in her voice. She pushed Tiga behind the back of Mavis's stall. 'Come on, hurry up, Tiga. We need to finish this documentary.'

'You're being weird,' Tiga said. 'Very weird.'

The jam stall looked small from the outside, piled high with jam jars and peppered with cats, but once you stepped behind it and peered past the frayed curtain at the back, it was as big as a big house!

'Yeah,' Mavis said with a shrug. 'This is my house.'

Tiga slid inside, where witches were sitting around a cosy kitchen table filling jars with freshly made jam straight from an old cauldron. The roof had a huge crack down the middle.

'Did someone break the roof?' Tiga asked as she turned to see Fluffanora frantically shaking her head at Mavis. As soon as she saw Tiga looking at her, she stopped.

'... No,' Mavis said slowly, not taking her eyes off Fluffanora.

'But it looks cracked,' Tiga said, pointing at it.

'Only you break my roof, Tiga,' Mavis said with a nervous giggle.

This was true. When Tiga had first landed in Sinkville, she'd landed smack bang on top of Mavis's roof. And she'd been accidentally falling on it and breaking it ever since.

'And you haven't been anywhere near Mavis's roof,' Fluffanora said quickly, making a show of opening her trunk and pulling clothes out of it as if to distract Tiga.

In the corner was a stack of jam jars shaped like shoes.

'Please don't say you're trying to make jam jar *shoes*,' Fluffanora said.

Mavis blinked. 'OK.'

'I'll do this interview,' Fran said, flying over to Mavis as Lizzie Beast lumbered after her.

'Mavis,' Fran said seriously. 'Why do you like jam?'

Mavis pondered the question for a moment. 'I don't actually like jam. It's disgusting.'

'But,' Fran spluttered, 'you're Ritzy City's biggest jam seller!'

'Exactly,' Mavis said with a shrug. 'That's a very different thing to being Ritzy City's biggest jam *eater*.'

'Who is Ritzy City's biggest jam eater?' Fran asked, her voice lowered.

'Fluffanora, definitely,' Mavis said, winking in her direction.

'YES!' Fluffanora said, punching the air. 'I knew it was me.'

'So you hate jam?' Fran asked Mavis again.

'Yes.'

'You'd never eat it?'

'No.'

'Why did you start selling jam then?'

'Accident.'

'Accident?'

'My latest thing was not an accident,' Mavis said proudly. 'I've created jam jar bags! The new Witchoween craze – no party is complete without them!'

Fluffanora draped one over her shoulder. 'I like these!'

Mavis's eyes lit up. 'AND MY NEXT IDEA IS THAT WE COULD MAKE THEM CAT-SHAPED.'

'No, Mavis,' Fluffanora said sternly. 'Stop trying to make everything cat-shaped.'

Five Things You Didn't Know About Mavis, by Tiga

1. Mavis never misses an episode of *Cooking for Tiny People* and recently got a ticket to sit in the live studio audience! But she got kicked out for throwing a peach.

2. She can speak eight languages – four witch ones, four human ones.

3. Every morning she delivers a fresh pot of jam to Peggy, along with a nice note or a drawing.

4. Every week she meets up with Crispy for a Trilly's tea and a chat. Crispy is her favourite fairy.

5. Her least successful jam product was a jam face cream, which made people look injured.

How to Make a Jam Jar Party Bag

WHAT YOU'LL NEED:

- ☆ An empty jam jar with a lid
- ☆ Ribbon
- ☆ Glue pen
- ☆ Glitter
- ☆ Bowl

HOW TO MAKE IT:

1. Take the jam jar lid and ask an adult to pierce two holes in it (they don't need to be a witch, but a magic adult human will do it a lot more quickly than a normal adult, who will probably have to use scissors and skewers and things like that).

2. Thread the ribbon through the holes and tie together on the underside of the lid so it makes a ribbon handle.

3. Take the glue pen and draw cool patterns on the outside of the jar.

4. Pour glitter into a bowl.

5. Gently roll the jam jar in the glitter so it sticks to your glue drawings.

6. Leave the jar to dry overnight.

7. Fill with fun things for your guests – sweets, little funny notes, anything!

8. Screw on the lid and swing it by the handle – it's ready to go!

Linden House

It was getting dark by the time they'd emerged from Mavis's jam stall, and Linden House was glowing brightly – because of a giant, flashing WITCHOWEEN sign that was hanging, squint, right across the front of the building. Tiga tingled with excitement – her first Witchoween! It was almost time.

'You're back!' Peggy cried, racing outside and giving Tiga a hug.

Fluffanora marched past, lugging her trunk. Tiga spotted her wink at Peggy.

'What is going on?' Tiga asked. 'You're both up to something.'

Peggy's cheeks flushed. 'No we're not.'

Pat the chef peeked her head around the door. 'The

tarts are *finally* done – I put a spell on them to ban them from burning, and it worked. Shall I put them out before or after the big –' She stopped as soon as she saw Tiga.

'The big what?' Tiga asked.

'Nothing,' Fluffanora said as Pat the chef scuttled back inside.

'Anyway,' Peggy said with an excited squeak in her voice. 'You've still got to do *my* interview for *Witch Snitch*. Tiga, why don't you bring that notebook into the grand hall ...'

SURPRISE!

Tiga couldn't believe her eyes when she saw it. The grand hall, usually bare and full of echoes, was crammed full of witches from all over Sinkville! A huge neon HAPPY WITCHOWEEN, TIGA sign hung from the ceiling. Witches swung jam jar bags, and huge trays of Clutterbucks cocktails magically glided past. In the corner a bunch of witches were playing the Coves cake game.

'It's for you!' Peggy said as she and Fluffanora hugged Tiga tightly, knocking her over completely. 'Your first ever Witchoween!'

'I think we can all agree I was the best at not ruining the surprise,' Fran said. 'There are three things that I am particularly excellent at – surprises, singing and accessorising with feathers.'

'And there's more,' Fluffanora said, racing over to the window and flicking her finger.

The huge silky black curtains that covered the windows disappeared with a pop, and outside –

'Is that …' Tiga said, moving closer so she could get a better look.

Mavis was jumping up and down next to something crumpled on the ground by her jam stall.

'It's you, Tiga!' Fluffanora said. 'We had a statue made of you.'

'Where the first Tiga landed in Sinkville,' Felicity Bat said, her face emotionless.

'That's what I tripped over earlier!' Tiga said with a snort.

'We'd done an invisible spell to hide it,' Peggy explained. 'Well, Felicity did the spell.'

'That's why you've been weird, Fluffanora,' Tiga said with a grin. 'Because of this party, because of that statue!'

Fluffanora nodded. 'I thought you were going to figure it out.'

'You thought I was going to figure out that you were making a statue of me in a crumpled heap after falling from the sink pipes?'

'You are a good guesser,' Peggy said seriously.

'Well, it's … lovely,' Tiga said with a smile. 'But I fell on the roof of Mavis's jam stall, remember. Not the pavement.'

'We tried it on the roof of the jam stall,' Felicity Bat said, 'but it broke it. So we went with the pavement instead. Slightly historically inaccurate, but Peggy doesn't seem to care about these things.'

'That's why Mavis's roof was cracked and everyone was being weird when I brought it up!' Tiga said. 'It all makes sense now!'

'And do you know why we chose today?' Peggy asked.

Fran shoved a witch-sized tart in her mouth. 'Mits min mon mear!'

Tiga stared at them blankly.

'It's been ONE WHOLE YEAR since you fell from the weird human world above the pipes and into ours!' Peggy cheered.

The crowd of witches in the room cheered, too.

Mavis let out a delayed and distant 'yay' from beside the statue outside, before tottering in to join the party.

'Can you believe it's been a whole year since we met, right out there – you all terrified, me with gloopy hair,' Peggy said, squeezing Tiga tightly. 'When better to

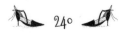

celebrate Witchoween this year than on the day I met my favourite witch!'

The crowd cheered and clinked their Clutterbucks glasses.

'This is … INCREDIBLE,' Tiga said, spinning in the room. 'And look at all the wonderful things! Cakes, Pies and That's About It Really tarts, sparkling outfits inspired by Desperate Dolls, bunting from the Mermaid Museum! Marge Mustoyd tights! Jam jar goodie bags!'

'The melting Miss Heks cheese bites were my idea,' Felicity Bat said.

'They are very you,' Tiga said with a smile.

Felicity Bat bowed her head proudly as someone behind her held up one of the Miss Heks cheese bites and screamed.

'To Tiga!' Peggy cried. 'Who changed my life.'

'You changed my life too,' Fluffanora said.

'And mine,' Fran said grandly and with a twirl.

Peggy kicked Felicity Bat's boot. 'Ow, Peggy. Ugh,' she said, rolling her eyes. 'You probably changed mine a bit, too.'

241

'She rid you of evil,' Fran quietly snapped at Felicity Bat. 'Show some respect.'

Felicity Bat rolled her eyes again.

'She certainly changed my jam stall!' Mavis added. 'More than once ... you know, because of all the falling on it and smashing it.'

'Yes, thank you, Mavis,' Peggy said.

'SPEECH!' one of the Cove witches yelled. 'SPEECH! SPEECH! SPEECH!'

Tiga stepped forward. Her mum waved at her, beaming.

'Thank you so much for this. In one year, I've realised I can levitate a bit, do spells, find long-lost mothers, fight off power-hungry lunatics, stop Fran from exploding ... I've realised I am a witch – and I can do anything.

'To Sinkville!' she cheered. 'TO MY FAVOURITE, FABULOUS WITCHES!'

'AND FAIRIES!' Fran shouted. 'For the love of a cat in a crumpled hat, when will you witches stop forgetting about THE FAIRIES?!'

Five Things You Didn't Know About Tiga, by Tiga (for fun)

1. She thinks Witchoween is the best thing ever. (Tiga also really likes writing about herself in her own notebook in third person.)

2. She accidentally knocked the skirt off the lamp post outside Brew's and now Lanky Lorna looks a bit naked.

3. She really wants to see *A Human Called Greg* at the Ritzytwig Theatre.

4. She secretly finds Fran hilarious, but can never tell her because it would only encourage her.

5. She thinks Witchoween is the best thing ever.

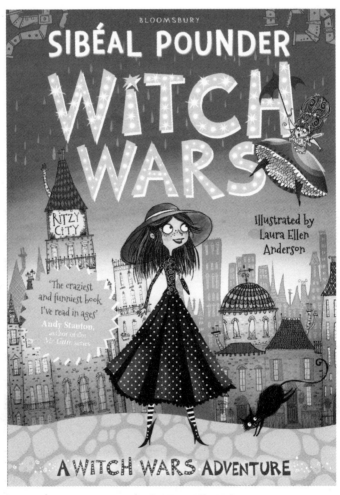

BLOOMSBURY

SIBÉAL POUNDER

WITCH WARS

RITZY CITY

Illustrated by
Laura Ellen
Anderson

'The craziest
and funniest book
I've read in ages'
Andy Stanton,
author of the
Mr Gum series

A WITCH WARS ADVENTURE

Read on for a peek at
the first WITCH WARS adventure

AVAILABLE NOW!

Down the Plughole

It would have been very difficult to spot Fran the fairy on the day this story begins. Her dress may have been puffy, her hair may have been huge, but she was barely the size of a small potato.

Fran was slowly sidestepping across a garden lawn, holding a large, limp leaf in front of her. She didn't want the owner of the garden to see her because Miss Heks was a terrible old woman with a grim face and size eleven shoes. If she had seen Fran she would've squashed her immediately.

Fran and her leaf were on a mission. There was something very important in the shed at the bottom of Miss Heks's garden. That something was a girl called Tiga Whicabim.

'You!' Tiga said, pointing at a slug that was sliding its way across an old stone sink. 'You will be the star of my show! You will play the role of Beryl, an ambitious dancer with severe hiccups.'

Tiga had been in the shed for hours. The evil Miss Heks had been her guardian for as long as Tiga could remember and she had quickly learned to keep out of her way. If she didn't, the old bat would make her sew up the holes in her disgusting, scratchy dresses. Or she would force Tiga to run up and down the garden in her gigantic, ugly shoes, bellowing things like 'FASTER!' and 'OH, DID YOU TRIP?' from the kitchen window.

Tiga shone a torch on the slug.

'You are going to be the best actor the world has ever seen!' she cried.

Fran sighed when she saw that.

Not because she'd finally found Tiga, after a long and perilous journey that had almost ended with her being eaten by a dog.

No, the reason Fran sighed was because she loved a bit of acting!

Despite her small size, Fran was a big deal in the world of show business. Everyone called her Fran the Fabulous Fairy (a name she had made up for herself). She had hosted many award-winning TV shows like *Cooking for Tiny People* and *The Squashed and the Swatted* and she'd played the lead role in *Glittery Sue* – a tragic drama about a small lady called Sue who got some glitter in her hair and couldn't get it out again.

'An actor you say!' Fran said, making Tiga jump.

Tiga stared, mouth open, at the small person that marched across the shed and – very ungracefully, and with much grunting – climbed up the leg of her trusty old rocking chair.

Fran stretched out a hand.

'Very delighted to meet you, Tiga! Now, it's pronounced *Teega*, isn't it? That's what I thought! I'm very good at names and absolutely everything else. I'm Fran the Fabulous Fairy. But you can call me Fran. Or Fabulous. BUT NEVER JUST FAIRY. I hate that.'

Tiga, understandably, assumed she had gone mad. Or at the very least fallen asleep.

She squinted at the little thing with big hair and then looked to the slug for reassurance, but it was sliding its way across the floor as if it knew exactly who Fran was, and was trying to escape.

'I don't think,' Fran said, pointing at the slug, 'that she should be acting in the lead role. She is slimy and not paying much attention.'

Fran wiggled a foot and a beehive of hair just like her own appeared on top of the slug's head.

'Much, much, *much* better,' she said.

Tiga panicked – the slug had *hair*! Not any old hair, a beehive of perfectly groomed hair! It was a split-second reaction, but with a flick of her hand she batted the fairy clean off the rocking chair.

Fran wobbled from left to right and tried to steady herself.

'Did you just *swat* me?' she snapped. 'The ultimate insult!'

Tiga tried to avoid eye contact and instead looked at

the slug. She couldn't be sure, but it looked a lot like it was shaking its head at her.

'WITCHES ARE NOT ALLOWED TO SWAT FAIRIES. IT IS THE LAW,' Fran ranted.

'I'm sorry!' Tiga cried. 'I didn't think you were real – I thought you were just my imagination! You don't need to call me a witch.'

'Yes I do,' said Fran, floating in front of Tiga with her hands on her hips. 'Because you are one.'

'I am one what?' Tiga asked.

'One witch,' said Fran as she twirled in the air, got her puffy dress caught in her wings and crash-landed on the floor.

'BRAAAAT!' came a bellow from across the garden. 'Time to leave the shed. Your dinner is ready!'

Tiga glanced nervously out of the window. 'If you are real, although I'm still not convinced you are, you'd better leave now. Miss Heks is a terrible old woman and she will do horrible, nasty, ear-pinching things to you.'

Fran ignored her and went back to twirling in the air. 'What are you having for dinner?'

'Cheese water,' Tiga said with a sigh. 'It's only ever cheese water.'

Fran thought about this for a moment. 'And how do you make this cheese water?'

'You find a bit of mouldy old cheese and you put it in some boiling water,' said Tiga, looking ill.

Fran swooped down lower and landed on the sink. 'Well, I'm afraid we don't have cheese water in Ritzy City – it's mostly cakes.'

Tiga stared at the fairy. 'Ritzy where?'

'*Riiiitzzzzzy Ciiiiity!*' Fran cheered, waving her hands in the air.

Tiga shrugged. 'Never heard of it.'

'But you're a witch,' said Fran.

'I am not a witch!' Tiga cried.

'You SO are!'

'I am not!'

'Definitely are,' said Fran, nodding her head. 'Even your name says so.'

And with that she flicked her tiny finger, sending a burst of glittery dust sailing across the room.

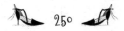

250

TIGA WHICABIM, the dust read.

Then it began to wobble and rearrange itself into something new.

I AM A BIG WITCH.

'You've cheated somehow,' Tiga mumbled, moving the dust letters about in the air. Most people would've believed Fran by this point, but Tiga wasn't used to magic and fun and insane fairies. So, despite this very

convincing evidence that she might just be a witch, Tiga still walked towards the door. Towards the cheese water.

'TIGA!' bellowed Miss Heks. 'YOUR CHEESE WATER HAS REACHED BOILING POINT.'

'Cheese water,' Fran chuckled. 'Wait! Where are you going, Tiga?'

'To eat dinner,' said Tiga. 'Bye, Fabulous Fairy Fran. It was lovely to meet you.'

Fran raised a hand in the air. 'Wait! *What?* You're not coming with me to Ritzy City, a place of wonder and absolutely no cheese?'

Tiga paused. Even if it was a mad dream, it was better than cheese water. She turned on her heel and walked back towards Fran.

Fran squealed and squeaked and did somersaults in the air.

'WHAT'S GOING ON IN THERE? I KNOW YOU CAN HEAR ME, YOU LITTLE MAGGOT!' Miss Heks shouted.

Tiga could see Miss Heks stomping her way towards the shed.

'Quick!' Fran cried. 'We must go to Ritzy City right now!'

'*How?*' Tiga cried, frantically looking around the shed for an escape route.

'Down the sink pipes, of course,' Fran said as she shot through the air and straight down the plughole.

'Come on, Tiga!' her shrill little voice echoed from somewhere inside the sink.

Tiga leaned over the stone sink and stared down the plughole.

There was nothing down there. No light. And certainly no city, that was for sure.

The door to the shed flew open and splinters of old wood went soaring through the air.

'WHAT IS GOING ON?' Miss Heks bellowed.

'NOW!' Fran yelled.

Tiga wiggled a finger in the plughole.

This is nonsense, she thought, just as she disappeared.

Ritzy City

Tiga slid down the pipe at a slug's pace.

It was not magical.

She had imagined if anything was going to happen it would be slick – something with a little *whoosh*. Instead it was more of a *smoosh*. With her cheeks squashed against the sides of the pipe, she squeaked her way very slowly to somewhere else. That somewhere else was Ritzy City, because although Fran may have been a bit mad she was no liar.

Tiga slipped out of the pipe, fell through a layer of thick black clouds and let out a yelp as she landed with a thud on the roof of a small market stall.

'An impressive landing!' Fran shouted as Tiga peeled her face off the soft canvas roofing. 'NO BROKEN

BONES OR DEATH! WELL DONE.'

Tiga blinked as her eyes shifted from the fairy flying in front of her face to what lay beyond.

For as far as she could see, everything was black and grey. There wasn't a drop of colour in the place. Even Fran's dress had changed from purple to a deep dark grey. But it wasn't all black and grey in a horrible way, like the shed at night. It was beautiful. Black fluffy clouds with soft grey edges hung in the sky. The pavements were lined with smart black market stalls that stretched as far as Tiga could see. Behind the stalls towered buildings built in shiny black stone that went up and up and disappeared into the clouds. From those clouds came trickles of water. But it wasn't rain. Tiga imagined it might be what rain looked like if someone forgot to turn it off properly.

She jumped down off the stall roof and peered out from behind it.

Further down the road, huge black vases held delicate grey flowers and little pruned shrubs sat proudly outside the gleaming black doors of townhouses

trimmed with black polished railings. And all along the street women marched about in the most magnificent dresses of every possible shape and fabric – silk, chiffon, velvet, long, short, puffy. And every woman in every dress wore the same wide-brimmed black hat.

Tiga just stood there with a huge, dozy grin slapped on her face. Ritzy City was the most incredible city she had ever seen.

'Oh dear,' said Fran as a woman pushing a sparkly black cannon pulled up next to them. 'Tiga … you might just want to cover your ear–'

'NEWS FLASH!' the woman bellowed as the cannon spun to face the sky and …

BANG!

Tiga dived to the ground.

When she looked up, hundreds of bits of paper were slowly floating back down to earth.

'Is that … ?' she began.

'It's the *Ritzy City Post*, our daily newspaper,' Fran said as a copy landed on Tiga's head.

WITCH WARS BEGINS TOMORROW was stamped on the front page.

Tiga raised the paper in the air. 'What's Witch Wars? Where exactly are we? And why is that woman allowed to wander around town firing a *cannon*?'

Fran opened her mouth to answer, but the witch manning the stall on which Tiga had fallen interrupted them.

'Hello, I'm Mavis. Jam?'

Tiga shyly shook her head.

'But witches love jam,' said Fran. 'They can't get enough of it.'

'That's why all these stalls sell jam,' said Mavis. 'Apart from that one at the end. It sells cats *and* jam.'

Tiga got to her feet and dusted herself off. 'I'm not a witch, Fran. I don't care if my name says so.'

'Everyone's a witch!' said Mavis, organising her jam jars in a neat row. 'Well, everyone here at least.'

258

Tiga watched the women striding past her. They didn't look anything like witches.

'The hats are wrong for a start,' she thought aloud. 'Why aren't they pointy? The tops are completely flat and not witch-like at all.'

'Ah ha!' said Fran, twirling in the air. 'That means you've only seen a witch up there above the pipes in *your* world. When a witch travels up there, although frog knows why they'd want to, they're sucked up the pipes, you see. It destroys the hat, making it all pointy. And some witches get horrible warts on their faces from all the grime – it depends on the condition of the pipe they travel in. Some knock their noses and it makes them crooked. Their dresses become all torn and tattered. Pipe travel is a horrible business.'

Mavis handed Tiga a tissue. 'You've not done too badly, only a bit of slime on your cheeks.'

Tiga grabbed the tissue and started madly rubbing her face.

'I thought you were going to be one of those ones whose nose goes all warty,' Fran chuckled.

'What about the water?' Tiga asked. 'It's not rain, is it?'

'No,' said Fran, watching trickles fall from the dark clouds. 'It comes from houses where you'll find a witch, up there in the world above the pipes. Some of them don't even know they're witches,' she added, with an eyebrow raised.

Tiga sighed. It was becoming very clear that there was no arguing with Fran.

'Right, we'd best be off or we'll be late,' Fran said, clicking her fingers in Tiga's face. And with that they waved goodbye to Mavis and her jam, and made their way along the bustling city street.

'So this is Ritzy Avenue,' Fran explained, while perched on Tiga's shoulder. 'It's the main shopping street. Over here we have Cakes, Pies and That's About It Really, the baker's. They make beautiful cakes and pies and That's It Really, which is a special type of tart only available in Ritzy City. *Very* delicious.'

Tiga pressed her hands up against the window and stared open-mouthed at the cakes, but just beyond

them, further into the shop, was a very peculiar scene. Inside, all the witches were staring, open-mouthed, back at her.

'Oh, and over there,' Fran said with a squeak of excitement as she pulled on Tiga's hair, 'is Brew's designer clothes shop. I love it! They make special dresses for me because I'm quite fabulous and famous, and also abnormally small. Mrs Brew is Ritzy City's best fashion designer, but you almost never see her. She spends most of her time in that studio up there.' Fran nodded towards a large round window at the very top of Brew's.

Tiga was almost certain she saw the shadow of someone walk past it. Then a chattering line of ladies burst out of the door and trotted down the street carrying black bags stamped with a huge swirly 'B'.

'Cool,' Tiga said, heading towards the door.

'No time for clothes shopping!' Fran said, zooming on ahead. Tiga reluctantly scuttled after her. She didn't want to lose the only person she knew in Ritzy City.

Fran screeched to a halt outside the most beautiful

townhouse Tiga had ever seen. And she had seen three townhouses.

'This is Linden House,' said Fran.

Tiga felt small and insignificant next to the huge building. On it there was a gigantic sign covered in lights that read WITCH WARS, and below it hung nine huge flags. On them were nine huge faces. Tiga didn't recognise any of them, apart from the last one.

It was her.

Read the whole ritzy, glitzy, witchy series!

AVAILABLE NOW!

Dear Honorary Witches
Above the Pipes!

© Richard Grassie

    Thank you very much for reading this book. I really hope you enjoyed it and Fran wasn't too unbearable.
FRAN IS THE BEST THING IN THIS BOOK. AND EVERYONE THINKS SO.*

    Chances are, if you're reading a book, you really like stories, and – if you're anything like me – you probably like making them up and writing them down too.

    A lot of the stuff in this book I made up when I was about seven or eight. I used to peer down the plughole and say, 'We just don't know what's down there.' But I loved witches, so I imagined a huge, weird witchy world below the pipes – and that's where the idea for Sinkville came from!

    (I also imagined Fran shooting out of the plughole and pinching my nose when I was brushing my teeth.)
BEST THING YOU EVER IMAGINED.*

    So if you have story ideas, or imagine characters and weird worlds, keep hold of them! Write them down! Never forget them, because your ideas are brilliant. And who knows? One day, you might want to make your ideas into a book.

Witchy wishes, AND GLITTERY DUST!*

Sibéal

*Sibéal's letter may have been edited by Fran.